A magical academy. A suspicious death. Can an inexperienced cop expose the deadly secrets lurking behind bewitched classroom doors?

Download Saved by the Spell for FREE to solve a mystical murder today!

ERIN JOHNSON

ENGLISH AFTER-DOOM TEA

A MAGICAL TEA ROOM MYSTERY

OTHER BOOKS BY ERIN JOHNSON

The Magical Tea Room Mysteries

Minnie Wells is working her marketing magic to save the coziest, vampire-owned tea room in Bath, England. But add in a string of murders, spells to learn, and a handsome Mr. Darcy-esque boss, and Minnie's cup runneth over with mischief and mayhem.

Spelling the Tea
With Scream and Sugar
A Score to Kettle
English After-Doom Tea

The Spells & Caramels Paranormal Cozy Mysteries

Imogen Banks is struggling to make it as a baker and a new witch on the mysterious and magical island of Bijou Mer. With a princely beau, a snarky baking flame and a baker's dozen of hilarious, misfit friends, she'll need all the help she can get when the murder mysteries start piling up.

Seashells, Spells & Caramels
Black Arts, Tarts & Gypsy Carts

Mermaid Fins, Winds & Rolling Pins
Cookie Dough, Snow & Wands Aglow
Full Moons, Dunes & Macaroons
Airships, Crypts & Chocolate Chips
Due East, Beasts & Campfire Feasts
Grimoires, Spas & Chocolate Straws
Eclairs, Scares & Haunted Home Repairs
Bat Wings, Rings & Apron Strings
* Christmas Short Story: Snowflakes, Cakes & Deadly Stakes

The Magic Market Paranormal Cozy Mysteries

A curse stole one witch's powers, but gave her the ability to speak with animals. Now Jolene helps a hunky police officer and his sassy, lie-detecting canine solve paranormal mysteries.

Pretty Little Fliers
Friday Night Bites
Game of Bones
Mouse of Cards
Pig Little Lies
Breaking Bat
The Squawking Dead
The Big Fang Theory

The Winter Witches of Holiday Haven

Running a funeral home in the world's most merry of cities has its downsides. For witch, Rudie Hollybrook, things can feel a little isolating. But when a murder rocks the festive town, Rudie's special skills might be the one thing that can help bring the killer to justice!

Cocoa Curses
Solstice Spirits

Magical Renaissance Faire Mysteries

Trapped in a magical Renaissance Faire and accused of murder. Huzzah!

When Adelaide "Laidey" Ryan dragged herself off the couch for a date at the Renaissance Faire, she didn't expect to run into her cheating ex-fiancé. The day only gets better when she winds up trapped on the magical grounds and discovers she's a witch. And the best part? She's charged with a homicide she didn't commit.

Much A'Broom About Nothing

Special Collections

The Spells & Caramels Boxset Books 1-3

Pet Psychic Mysteries Boxset Books 1-4

Pet Psychic Mysteries Boxset Books 5-8

Want to hang out with Erin and other magical mystery readers?

Come join Erin's VIP reader group on Facebook: **Erin's Bewitching Bevy**. It's a cauldron of fun!

1

OFF TO THE RACES

"And they're off!"

I paused to watch the horses thunder by on the track far below. It was day one of the Derbyshire jump races, and all eyes were either glued to the track, visible through the clear plastic siding, or one of the half a dozen television screens around our tent that showed the race unfolding. The shouting and screaming raised to an almost deafening volume, and though I wasn't a fan, the hairs on my arms stood on end at the pure energy and excitement.

The announcer's voice resonated with passion over the loudspeakers, rattling off at a speed almost as quick as the horses.

"And Jane Austen and Little Grey Goose are neck and neck coming round the bend! It's a shocker! Little Grey Goose takes the lead!"

With the horses out of sight on the track, I glanced up at the television. Jane Austen was the beautiful black mare tearing down the field. Apparently, she was a big deal and the horse favored to take the Derbyshire Cup this year, though at the moment she was squarely in the middle of the pack.

Jane Austen (the horse) was also the reason I was helping my vampire boss, Fitz, and his butler employees serve this weekend. I'd landed the Bath Butler Cafe, for which I ran marketing, this prestigious gig catering one of the biggest marquees at the races by pitching the cafe's connection to Jane Austen (the author). The track loved it, and I'd volunteered to go away to Derbyshire for the weekend with the guys. One, it'd be a nice change of scenery, and two, in case we got swamped, I'd be here to help serve. Fitz had lived his prime years during the Regency (before he was turned) and so he'd themed his business according to the time period in which he felt most at home. The tearoom prided itself on manners and period outfits and even featured Jane Austen-themed names for our teas and baked goods. We'd brought our delicious tea, scones, finger sandwiches, and signature Regency style to the races—and so far it'd been a hit with the posh crowd. They gushed over the food—who wouldn't; Fitz was an amazing baker—and reveled in being bowed and catered to.

I bit my lip, nervous, as the horses bounded over the final hurdle and rounded the corner toward the last stretch, with the gray horse inching farther and farther in front of Jane Austen. As the horses dashed across the finish line, the crowd in the stands below us jumped to their feet, the shouting a mixture of boos and cheers.

The mood in the makeshift marquee tearoom was slightly more subdued, but an older gentleman loudly scoffed, while a woman in an enormous flower-covered hat slammed her cup down so hard it rattled in the saucer.

Dominik, his arms laden with empty plates, sidled up beside me. "Someone bet on the wrong horse."

I chuckled.

Dom was enormous—tall and beefy—with chiseled features and pouty lips. I'd come to view all the butlers like brothers, but I was probably the only woman at the races who wasn't sighing over his good looks—and I didn't blame them.

"I'm guessing quite a few people are out *a lot* of money." He leaned close, his eyes glued to one of the screens, and I followed his gaze. On the television, the young woman on the winning horse ducked her head as an older blond woman slipped a floral wreath around her neck and then embraced her. An ecstatic circle of jumping and cheering men and women surrounded the two women and the gray horse.

Dom jerked his chin at the screen. "That was a big upset. Jemma Watkins and her mum, the one who just wreathed her, are clearly thrilled. Jemma's a bit of a media darling. They'll eat this up."

Journalists shoved microphones at the grinning young woman on the horse as camera flashes lit up her face.

I glanced at Dom with raised brows. "Her mum?"

He jerked his chin at the screen. "Cindy Watkins. She's a big name; local breeder."

I nodded, not quite sure what that all meant, but the Watkinses were clearly a talented family when it came to horses.

Dom scoffed, and I followed his gaze back to the television. The young man who'd ridden the favored black horse, Jane Austen, dismounted, only to be accosted by a furious older guy. Though we couldn't hear the audio, the bald man shouted, his face red and contorted, while the young jockey just hung his head, wincing.

I frowned, concerned for the young man being berated. "Who is that?"

"Samar Chopra."

I frowned, recognizing the name. He and his famous horse had been plastered all over the papers and promos for the races. "Not the jockey… I meant the guy yelling at him."

Dom snorted. "Timmy Pipe. He's a legendary horse trainer, worked with over a dozen grand champions. I don't blame him for being pissed—I mean, Jane Austen was a shoo-in to win—but he's also known for his temper." He sucked in a breath over his teeth. "I would *not* like to be in Samar Chopra's boots right now."

Dominik started toward the makeshift kitchen in the back.

I started after him. "Wait—does that mean Jane Austen is just out, now?"

I wasn't big into horse racing, but Jane Austen happened to be my favorite author, and our marquee was themed for both her and the horse. I couldn't help but root for her.

Dom winced. "Yep. Jemma and Little Grey Goose will be advancing to the finals for the Cup."

Feeling somewhat disappointed for poor Jane Austen, I followed Dom to the back. We shared a makeshift kitchen space between our tent and the marquee next door, which was being catered by an upscale restaurant.

The narrow space was a flurry of activity, with the restaurant's waiters bustling in and out with orders. Fitz stood nearly back-to-back with a striking woman, probably a decade older than I was, in her late thirties. She wore a white chef's jacket, her long black hair braided down her back.

As Dom and I deposited our plates by the sink, where Calvin was on dish duty, I snuck a glance at my handsome vampire boss. His dark brows were pulled close together as his large, flour-covered hands deftly piped macarons. He frowned with concentration, a single wavy lock of dark hair falling over his forehead.

Fitz and I had been flirting for months now, but his reserved Regency manners kept things moving at a slow pace. Which, honestly, was for the best. I was freshly out of an ugly divorce and not sure my heart had fully healed enough to get serious with anyone again. Though lately, with the summer nights warm and couples strolling along the Avon hand in hand, I'd found myself yearning for a little romance.

The other chef, Carmen Corerro, backed up—right into Fitz. They both jumped, and she whirled around.

"My apologies," she gushed. Her dark eyes widened as she glanced at Fitz's pastries. "I hope I didn't make you ruin any of those—they look exquisite."

I curled my lip. Exquisite? I mean, I didn't disagree, but she was laying it on a little thick, wasn't she?

"It's quite alright." Fitz gave her a tight smile, then turned back to his work, but she placed a hand on his hairy forearm, and he glanced back.

"I understand you're a bit understaffed, so if you need *anything* from me, don't hesitate to ask."

I sniffed. We didn't need her help. We were doing just fine, thank you.

Fitz bowed his head. "Thank you for the gracious offer. I believe my staff is managing quite well at the moment, but I shall keep it in mind."

She batted her lashes at him, then turned back to her stove.

Fitz huffed and grumbled to himself as he glanced around the countertop. "Now where is that sifter?"

"You okay, Minnie?"

I blinked, startled out of glaring at Carmen.

Dominik grinned at me, a knowing look in his dark eyes.

"What?" I shrugged and grabbed the next order, a tea tray laden with finger sandwiches on freshly baked bread, cranberry scones with whipped honey butter, and strawberry macarons. "I'm fine."

"Sure."

He and Calvin exchanged grins, but I just rolled my eyes, my cheeks hot, and hustled back out into the marquee with the tea tray in my hands. It wasn't like Fitz and I were officially an item, but that Carmen was acting way over-the-top, fawning all over him like that. It didn't help that Fitz had been in an uncharacteristically grumpy mood all day.

The handsome vampire was stuck in his ways. It'd been an effort to get him to let me modernize his marketing efforts in the first place, but I appreciated his willingness to try. Still, the man dressed like it was 1810, and by our mutual friend Gus's account, Fitz basically spent all his time at his estate or the tearoom. Fitz liked to be in his element—and me setting up this weekend event was anything but.

While Fitz appreciated that it was a good opportunity to bring in new customers and spread the word about his tearoom in Bath, I suspected he was also discombobulated and cranky about the change to his routine. I could understand. Change could be hard. But my divorce had taught me that sometimes we have no choice but to change.

As I threaded through the round tables, draped in elegant white linens and topped with vases overflowing with bright flowers, a hand wrapped around my upper arm, startling me.

2

CHARMED, I'M SURE

I glanced down and to my left, then fought not to roll my eyes when I realized it was Gary Simms who'd grabbed hold of me. Gary had been the first one seated at nine o'clock this morning, as soon as our tent opened, and he'd only left long enough to head to the restroom a few times. He'd ordered a steady stream of drinks and food, and I feared we may have to kick him out when we closed up this evening, since he showed no signs of leaving.

I shifted on my feet and shot his hand a pointed look. "Yes?"

He finally released me and raised a single pudgy finger. "Another tea tray? Also, could I do another pitcher of those delicious mimosas?" He swayed in his seat, his cheeks flushed and eyes bloodshot. "Less orange juice though, this time." He gave me a staggered blink—maybe he'd tried to wink?

I gave him a tight smile and nodded. "Of course. Anything else?"

He dabbed at his balding head with a cloth napkin. "Did you see the big race?"

I glanced back through the clear plastic tarp that ran along one side of the tent and looked out over the track. "This last one?"

He nodded, which sent his neck wobbling. "Little Grey Goose won." He beamed.

"Did you bet on her?" Apparently, he was one of the few who were happy about the upset.

He sucked on his lips. "More than that. You know my tab?" He leaned forward as if sharing a great secret, and stage whispered, "Cindy Watkins is the one paying for it."

I blinked, surprised. "The horse breeder?" She was the mother of the jockey who'd ridden Little Grey Goose.

Gary nodded and waggled his brows. "I'm kind of a big deal."

He clearly wanted me to be impressed, but since I had no idea how Gary was involved with the winning team—and had no interest in sticking around to hear about it—I wasn't quite sure what to say.

"Oh, well... good for you both."

I started off, but he cleared his throat. "Ahem!"

I backstepped and raised a brow.

"Aren't you forgetting something?"

I searched my memory—had I forgotten part of his order?

He rolled his thick wrist and bent slightly forward.

Oh. I frowned as I realized he wanted me to do the customary line our butlers said, along with the bow. Only, I wasn't usually a butler, and our customers were typically sweet little old ladies or young women celebrating a bridal shower, not tipsy older dudes who were a little too handsy.

I stifled a sigh, bowed my head, and mumbled a half-hearted, “Your wish is my command.”

“Ah, love hearing that every time.” He rubbed his hands together, and I set my jaw as I moved off to deliver my tea tray. How did that man know Cindy Watkins, the breeder of the winning horse? And why on earth was she paying for his tab, especially when he was taking such advantage of her hospitality?

As I threaded between full tables, lifting my tray to squeeze between chairs, I thought over Gary’s words. He seemed a bit lonely (he’d been at the table by himself all day) and eager to brag. Maybe he just wanted me to *think* he was a VIP.

As I delivered the tray of sandwiches and goodies to the table of women in the corner, a familiar—and unexpected—face caught my eye.

I smiled at them and held up a finger. “Excuse me, I’ll be right back.”

I bowed my head, then darted out of the tent and into the stands, rising on tiptoe to glance over the heads (and enormous hats) of the dense crowd. The lush green fields stretched out below, interrupted only by the oval racetrack and a few white picket fences. I pulled my eyes from the horses and their riders, warming up with slow laps, and scanned the crowd.

A shock of wiry gray hair tumbled over the shoulders of a slight woman in one of the seats, the spots beside her empty aside from her patchwork quilt purse.

I climbed my way down the aisle until I reached her row. “Mim?”

The older witch turned around, her faint brows raised, then grinned as she spotted me. “Minnie!” She clasped her ring-covered hands together. “What a pleasant surprise.”

She patted the empty seat beside her, beckoning for me to join her. I slid down the row, apologizing as I climbed my way over others' feet, then perched on the hard plastic seat beside my magical mentor.

I'd been taking monthly magic lessons from Mim for about half a year now at her potions shop in Bath. I'd had no idea I'd find her an hour away in Derbyshire... at a horse race, of all places.

I shot her a puzzled look. "What are you doing here?"

She arched a brow. "What? Am I not allowed to have a day or two off?"

I raised my own brows. "You didn't mention you'd be heading to the races at our last lesson."

She played with the ends of her curly hair and grew airy. "Didn't I?"

I shook my head, my expression flat. "No."

"Oops." She shrugged.

"I just didn't take you for a horse racing fan." She was acting even more aloof and mysterious than normal. What was Mim up to?

She snorted. "Oh. I'm not." The older witch jerked her small, pointed chin behind me. "In fact, normally, you'd be more likely to find me on the other side of the entrance gates with those protestors."

I glanced down, recalling. "Oh, yeah. I saw them on the way in." There'd been a group of about fifteen men and women of all ages with picket signs at the entrance. "What's that about?"

Mim spun to face me more directly and lowered her voice. She smoothed her long, paisley skirt over her knee. "Penny Zhang's their leader. She was quite a famous jockey, but a couple of years ago her horse fell during one of the races here at Derbyshire and broke its leg."

She pressed her lips tight together. "It had to be put down."

My stomach twisted. "That's terrible."

"Tragic." She nodded. "And it's not at all uncommon." She pointed at me. "Did you know that on average, seven horses die during the three days of races here?"

"No." I recoiled. "Seriously?"

She raised her brows and nodded, her blue eyes wide. "Unbelievable, right? And that's not counting all the ones that are injured and killed during training." She tsked. "Poor creatures. Anyway, Penny Zhang quit jockeying and joined forces with the protestors after that."

I didn't blame her. That must've been traumatic, to lose her horse like that. I glanced toward the track down below us and curled my lip. The horses were being led to the starting line, and my stomach clenched at the thought that one of those beauties might get hurt—or even killed—just for the sport of all these people in the stands. Suddenly, I wasn't sure how to feel, being amongst them.

Which brought me back to Mim. "So... why are you here again?"

She lowered her voice so that I had to lean close to hear her over the blaring of the announcer on the loudspeaker and the din of conversation around us.

"I have a... *special* relationship with one of the track's veterinarians. He's aware of my abilities and allows me to visit the horses in the morning before the races, to cast protection spells over them."

I gaped. "Isn't that cheating?"

"Psht." She waved me off. "It's not to help them *win*, it's just to help keep the horses from getting injured."

I grinned. "Aw, that's really kind of you."

I already knew my mentor was a good person, but as an

animal lover, this endeared her to me even more. Ever since I'd discovered my powers, I'd struggled to find a coven where I fit in. Eventually, I'd given up—which meant learning to use my powers on my own from books and self-study. Not the easiest going—especially since I had a tendency to start rainstorms… inside.

But Mim had taken me under her wing, and with her help, I was finally learning to tap into—and control—my magic. A warm rush of gratitude for her washed over me.

The older witch patted my knee. "You know, you should help me." She nodded, as if it were already decided. "Meet me at the stables tomorrow at four, and I'll teach you some new charms."

I choked. "Four in the *morning*?"

"We've got to get up early, dear, to beat the grooms. And there are *lots* of horses to charm, so it'll be good practice for you."

I gaped at her, still thinking of the early start time, then looked toward the tearoom tent. While it'd be a great experience to see the horses up close and help keep them safe, not to mention all the magic practice I'd get, I still had to work all afternoon, with another twelve-hour day ahead of me tomorrow.

I grimaced. "I would, but I'm already working all day serving for Fitz."

Mim leaned forward in her seat, her eyes fixed on the horses at the starting line. "I charm them as they come down the track too, just for extra protection, so I'm sorry, pet, but I can't talk any longer. Have to concentrate now." She absentmindedly patted my knee again. "See you tomorrow morning, bright and early."

I sighed. Looked like I'd be getting up with the horses.

3

HORSING AROUND

It was still dark when my alarm went off at a quarter till four the next morning. I fumbled around for my cell, disoriented by the fact that I was in an unfamiliar inn, and not my attic room at my best friend, Gus's, townhouse in Bath. It took Tilda, my black cat familiar, batting me in the face to wake me up enough to shut the blaring alarm off.

Of course, she immediately curled back into a ball of fur, half hidden under the fluffy pillow, and went back to sleep. I yanked on a pair of jeans, nearly falling over in the process, pulled a comfy sweater over my head, and slipped into my trainers.

As I pulled my long, dark hair into a ponytail, I curled my lip at my familiar, her head buried in the sheets. "So I take it you're not coming with me this morning?"

I wasn't sure why I was waiting for a response. It's not like she talked back... unless she did.

A couple of months ago, I'd participated in a Spring Solstice celebration with a bunch of other witches. I'd offered a decorated egg to some magical standing stones and cast a spell, asking for my powers to grow. Tilda had gone over and given the egg a lick, and then a couple of nights later, I swore I'd heard her voice in my head.

I shot the lump of fur in my bed a flat look. That had probably just been *all* in my head, because it hadn't happened again in the months since. I had to admit, though, my powers *did* seem to be growing. Spell casting was getting easier, and it seemed more natural to tap into my magic. Good thing, too—I was going to need all the help I could get to charm a bunch of horses at this early hour.

I planted my hands on my hips, elbows wide. "I'm going to go perform some magic on some very important horses. I could really use some amplification here."

She wriggled further under the sheets.

I glared at her, though I couldn't quite stifle a grin at how cute she was. "Fine." Lazy cat. Then again, I was probably just jealous—I'd kill to be able to sleep in.

My feet throbbed as I trudged down the dark lane, away from the inn to the nearby track. I'd had a long day on my feet yesterday—and I had another one to look forward to. Though it was late summer, I kept my hands stuffed into my pockets against the chill of the early morning, my breath fogging the air. A few birds chirped in the towering trees that lined the dirt lane, and some ancient-looking low stone walls meandered alongside the path.

Though I longed to be back in my cozy bed at the inn, I had to admit the morning out in the countryside was beautiful—so peaceful and quiet. My footsteps and breath sounded loud in the hush. I could use some tranquility after the constant roar of the crowd and frantic shouting of the announcers yesterday. I yawned and blinked my watering eyes as the low roof of the stable came into view, silhouetted against the gray early dawn sky, with the curve of the track and stands behind it.

Two shadowy figures emerged from the darkness, lounging against the white picket fence up ahead. I hesitated a moment, until I recognized Mim's wiry tumble of hair. She stood in a quilted overcoat, her arms crossed against the morning chill as she chatted with the tall, older gentleman beside her. I guessed he was in his early seventies, and with his tanned skin and salt-and-pepper hair and beard, I figured this must be her veterinarian friend.

As I approached, they both looked up, and I waved. The man uncrossed his ankles, pulled his hand out of his denim coat jacket, and reached out to shake my hand.

"You must be the Minnie I've heard so much about."

I smiled and shook his rough, strong hand as Mim gestured between us.

"Minnie, meet Jack. Jack, Minnie."

Jack winked. "I hear you share the same talents as my Mim."

My Mim, huh?

My older witch friend giggled.

I gawked at her. Since when did Mim giggle? I was starting to suspect that they had more than just a friendship.

Jack tipped his head toward the huge stables behind him. "Best we get going, ladies." He unhitched the gate and held it for us, then latched it behind.

Dewy grass brushed against my ankles as we trekked across the sprawling fields, until we reached the low, but massive, wood stable. A middle-aged guard sat outside the entrance on a folding chair, bundled up in a baseball cap and thick jacket, both embroidered with a security logo. A single lamp shone a pool of light down on him and the table he sat at, lending him enough light to read a newspaper by.

Jack led the way and lifted his hand in greeting. "Morning, Paul."

The guard looked up over his newspaper and nodded in greeting. "Jack." His eyes darted to Mim and me, and he lowered his paper. "Guests today?"

The guard folded up his paper and set it beside a tall thermos as Jack grinned at Mim. "More like much-needed helpers."

The man grunted and slid a clipboard and pen toward us. "You'll all need to sign in."

Jack and Mim scribbled away on the gridded paper, and then it was my turn. As Jack and the guard chatted about the chilly weather, I wrote my name, the date, our time of arrival (could I write "way too early"?) and then signed my name, leaving the "sign out" line blank for now.

The guard, Paul, pulled the clipboard back towards him, then jerked his head toward the open barn doors. "Head on in."

Jack raised a hand in thanks, and we filed past the guard into the warm stable. It smelled comforting, of hay and animals, the heat a welcome relief from the cold outside. A corrugated tin roof ran low overhead, punctuated with skylights that let in the gray light of the morning.

A few wall lamps cast a golden glow, while ropes, shovels, and various instruments lined the wooden walls. Rows and rows of stalls stretched out before us in the massive stable.

I leaned close to Mim as we sauntered toward the first row of stalls. "We're not going to have to muck them, are we?"

The older witch shot me a flat look. "No. I told you, dear, we're here to *charm* the horses, not clean up after them."

Jack, his hands stuffed in the pockets of his jacket, gave

an approving nod. "And *I'm* here to make sure the horses are fit to run today."

Despite how tired I was, I couldn't help but be curious about what Jack's job entailed. "How do you know if they're healthy enough to race?"

Jack grabbed a clipboard that hung on a nail outside the first stall and flipped through the pages. "Oh, we check on lots of things." He glanced up and gestured to the clipboard.

"We have detailed records on each horse. We know how much they usually eat, their sleeping habits, any prior injuries, any little quirks... it's all in here. We double check what's written down with what we see the day of the race—multiple times, in fact—and make sure the horses aren't presenting any new injuries or behavior that might indicate that they're not well."

Jack unlatched the top half of the green dutch door and pulled it open, leaving the bottom half closed. The enormous brown horse inside walked slowly forward, snorting and grunting. Jack reached a rough hand out and gave the horse's nose a quick rub.

"So you check on all the horses in the morning?" I drummed my fingers on the low door. "But what if they get hurt later, before the race?"

He winked, then stepped around me, into the stall with the horse. "Good question. I examine all the horses again in the afternoon and keep a close watch on them once they're transferred from the inspection bar to the areas where they're saddled and mounted—even all the way to the starting line."

He patted the big brown horse and lifted its foreleg, examining the hoof. "If a horse bucks or kicks, for instance, it might result in an injury right up to the moment before the starting pistol. And if that happens, everything's paused for the horse to be checked out again and cleared to race."

The horse patiently allowed Jack to continue his examination.

Wow. There was so much to races that I'd never thought about. I was grateful that Jack prioritized the horses' health but couldn't help doubting that everyone felt that way.

"There's probably a lot of pressure from the jockeys' teams to let them race, right?"

Jack's bushy brows dropped low over his eyes as he grew grim. "More than you can imagine, lass."

Mim shot her friend a sympathetic look. "It wasn't your fault, Jack."

I looked between them, puzzled. *What* hadn't been his fault?

4

STABLE CONDITION

The grizzled veterinarian shook his head. "I should've fought Timmy harder. It's not happening again under my watch." He squared his shoulders, his round belly puffing out below his flannel shirt.

Jack walked over to the next stall and perused the clip-board as I sidled closer to Mim. "What was that about?"

My friend glanced behind me at the veterinarian, and then leaned close, lowering her voice to almost a whisper. The horse ducked its head between us, as if it, too, was listening in.

"Two years ago, this famous—I should say *infamous*—trainer, Timmy Pipe, fought Jack tooth and nail to allow one of the horses to run. Jack didn't think it was safe, but Timmy Pipe is notoriously hard-nosed. He threw a fit, and because he's kind of a big deal in the horse racing world, Jack's call got overturned and they let the horse run."

I frowned, my stomach tight. I had a feeling the story didn't end well. "What happened?"

Mim's eyes filled with pain. "It was awful. On one of the final jumps, the horse fell and broke its leg. Horses aren't like us; once they're injured it's very hard for them to heal and recover."

Mim looked down and toed the hay-covered ground with her boot. "The poor horse had to be put down."

I brought a hand to my mouth. "Oh, that's awful."

Mim pressed her lips tight together. "Jack's never forgiven himself... or Timmy Pipe, for that matter. It traumatized the jockey, Penny Zhang, too." She pointed at me. "She's the one I told you about yesterday—the one who's become a protestor."

I shook my head. How horrible. Not only for the poor horse who lost its life, but for Jack and Penny as well.

The name Timmy Pipe sounded familiar... I thought back to the races yesterday and then remembered Dominik had pointed him out to me on the television. He was the bald guy who'd been yelling at his jockey after Jane Austen failed to win the race. That, plus everything Mim had just told me, convinced me that I didn't like this Timmy Pipe guy.

Mim squeezed my shoulder. "You can see now why this job of charming the horses is so important. We want to prevent anything like that from happening again."

I nodded, more eager now to learn how to help these horses and keep them safe. Despite having to drag myself out of bed at the early hour, I now felt proud and excited to be able to help in a meaningful way. "Okay, so what do we do?"

Mim winked at me. "There's my girl." She turned back to the brown horse, who snorted and gently tossed its head. "Again, we're not charming them to win; we just want to keep them out of harm's way. We're basically just modifying a protection spell." She gave me a serious look. "You remember we went over those last month, right, pet?"

I fought not to roll my eyes. "Yes, I remember." I bit my lip. "Could you refresh my memory though?"

She chuckled and held both palms a few inches away from the horse's face. "You want to find the energy in your palms. It might feel tingly, or like pulsing. Once you tap into that, focus your energy there, and imagine creating a protective bubble around the horse. It may take the form of a hard shield, or maybe more of a gentle cloud, but either way the goal here is to protect the horse from harm or injury."

She raised her thin brows at me, then tossed her wiry gray hair back over her shoulder. "Sometimes it helps to focus the energy if you recite a little spell." She gestured at the horse as she stepped back. "Why don't you give it a try?"

I sucked in a deep breath and stepped forward. The horse blinked its long, dark lashes at me, and I couldn't help but smile back at it. I tentatively reached a hand up, and when it didn't try to bite me or knock my hand away, I gently rubbed its smooth nose and forehead. "Hello, beauty."

My stomach clenched at the mere thought of any harm befalling such a gorgeous animal. I sucked in a deep breath and blew it out shakily. I held my chilled hands near the horse's face, just as Mim had done, then closed my eyes and tried to tap into the sensations in my palms.

Not much happened at first.

But I kept breathing and kept waiting. Eventually, I sensed a bit of a tingle in my palms, and then more of a strong pulsing, throbbing. I focused on that feeling and sent more energy and magic to my palms. It felt as though they sort of filled and charged up, the pulsing becoming quicker, stronger. Once my palms felt full, I turned my focus to a spell. I made it up on the spot.

"You're very pretty horse,
I want to keep you safe of course,
So on all your runs and jumps today,
May magic keep all harm away."

A tingly warmth washed over my whole body, from the top of my head down to my toes, like stepping into a warm shower. And then as quickly as it had come, it whooshed through me, out my palms, and then was gone. I opened my eyes and turned to Mim, who beamed at me.

She gave an approving nod. "Well done, pet, well done." She nodded towards the horse. "Quite a strong charm you cast there."

I couldn't tell any difference in the horse, but I'd take her word for it. I grinned, feeling quite proud of myself... even a little giddy.

Mim lifted her small, pointed chin. "You must have a great teacher."

I shook my head at her as she walked, chuckling, past me to the next stall.

"One down, about a hundred to go."

My breath caught. Was she serious? Casting that spell had been a rush, but it also left me a little bit shaky and tired. It kind of felt like a caffeine crash.

Did Mim seriously charm all these horses by herself, every day of the races? I trailed behind her, with a newfound appreciation for her skills as a witch. Not to mention her stamina. She had to be in her sixties but had more energy than I did on a good day.

I followed her to the next stall, while Jack examined a horse a couple of doors down from us.

The dappled gray had just stuck her head out the opening when Jack let out a strangled cry. His clipboard clattered to the ground, and he staggered back, away from the stall, a weathered hand over his mouth. Mim and I exchanged wide-eyed looks, then dashed down the row to join him.

Mim gripped his arm. "Jack, are you alright?"

I followed his horrified gaze to the stable and approached the partly open door.

"Minnie! Don't!"

Jack's warning came too late. I stood in the doorway and gazed at the man sprawled on the ground inside the stall—blank eyes staring up at the ceiling, unmoving. A pool of red blood stained the hay near his bald head. I froze, my feet rooted and chest heaving, then whirled to face Mim and Jack. I pulled my phone from my pocket and with shaking hands dialed 999.

"I'm calling the police." My voice came out hoarse as the phone rang.

Jack lowered his hand from his mouth and gave me a nod. "Good thinking." He squeezed Mim's hand, then strode past me and knelt beside the man. Jack placed two fingers on his neck as I held my breath, waiting. After a long moment he looked up and shook his head.

"He's gone."

The emergency operator answered, and I put my phone on speaker. "What's your emergency?"

"We found a man—he's dead." I didn't like how often I had to make these calls lately.

“Please stay calm.”

My heart thundered in my chest as I waited for the operator’s instructions.

“Do you know the deceased?”

Jack’s nostrils flared. “It’s Timmy Pipe.”

5

TIMMY PIPE

By the time the two detectives arrived with half a dozen uniformed officers, the sun had fully risen and the horses were stomping and snorting in their stalls. The older, curt Detective Bennett, and the younger wide-eyed Detective Calle, who seemed much too innocent to be investigating a murder, introduced themselves.

Bennett's dark eyes seemed to look right through me, her stern demeanor all business. She struck me as someone who paid attention to details, from her wrinkle-free, perfectly pressed black suit to her short, curly crop, with not a hair out of place. Her partner, Detective Calle, looked younger than I was. She barely spoke, and when she did it was in a small, quiet voice. While Bennett was put-together and polished, Calle's blond hair stuck out at all angles from a messy bun.

While they struck me as a bit of an odd couple, I was just grateful that I didn't have to deal with Detective Prescott again. A couple months ago, we'd gone on a date together that ended with a murder. Not to mention, he seemed to be collaborating with a suspected vampire hunter.

It was because of this that I'd convinced my best friend and roommate, Gus, to get out of town and go visit a friend in Scotland while Fitz and I were working here in Derbyshire. Although Gus was a powerful vampire who was hundreds of years older than me (he always said it was rude of me to ask his age), I couldn't help but worry about his safety. I knew he could look after himself, but with me and Fitz gone, I didn't want him to risk having to face down a vampire hunter alone.

And here *I'd* stumbled onto a dead body. Oh, the irony.

Jack, Mim, and I all gave our statements, and the uniformed officers were just loading the deceased Timmy Pipe's body onto a stretcher when racing staff began to filter into the stables.

Despite the officers' best efforts to keep them away, a small crowd of concerned onlookers soon gathered.

"What's going on?"

I glanced to my left. A slight young man with dark, curly hair, tanned skin, and a riding helmet tucked under his arm slid to the front of the crowd. An older guy and two young men accompanied him.

A uniformed officer approached with his palms outstretched. "Sir, this is a crime scene. We're going to need you to back up and—"

The young man's eyes widened, and I recognized him from the race yesterday. He was the jockey who'd ridden the famous Jane Austen. The same jockey who'd been chewed out by his trainer... Timmy Pipe. Only unlike yesterday, his left eye was nearly swollen shut, a painful-looking purple bruise on his swollen cheekbone.

I bit my lip, my stomach tightening. This was going to be a terrible shock for him, and it looked like he'd already had a tough night.

The older man beside him pointed at the stable that had been cordoned off by the police. "Those are our horses! What's going on? Did someone hurt them?"

The uniformed officer glanced back over his shoulder at Detective Bennett, who looked mildly annoyed. "Best let them on through."

She beckoned the jockey and his team forward, then pointed at Timmy Pipe's body, which now lay on the stretcher in an unzipped black body bag. A few officers crouched beside his body. "Do you know this man?"

The dark-haired jockey turned ashen, and his eyelids fluttered. The two young men beside him cursed, and the older man dragged a hand down his face.

He shook his head. "That's Timmy Pipe. He's our head trainer." He turned to Detective Bennett and her younger partner with his brows pinched in concern. "I'm Ralph, the assistant trainer."

He thumbed at the young man who looked as though he was about to faint. "This is Samar Chopra, our jockey, and these two young men are grooms. We all worked under Timmy."

Detective Bennett folded her arms and swept her discerning gaze over Timmy's team. "What happened to your eye, Samar?" She touched her own cheekbone. "That's quite a shiner."

His throat bobbed, and he dipped his chin, as if to hide his face. "I, uh... I got up in the middle of the night and tripped." He coughed out a humorless chuckle.

Detective Bennett stared at him, eyes narrowed. Even I thought it sounded like a pretty weak excuse.

Detective Bennett studied him for a long moment, then jerked her head at Detective Calle. "This is my partner. I need all of you to give her your statements about your relationship to the deceased."

Detective Calle stepped forward, her smartphone in her hand, and began recording the conversation. She tucked a strand of blond hair behind her ear and blinked her huge blue eyes up at the assistant trainer. "When was the last time you saw the victim?"

Ralph glanced down at his dirty leather boots and shrugged. "Why, had to be the same time the rest saw him." He glanced over his shoulder at the two young grooms and Samar, who all nodded their agreement, though the jockey still looked like he was either about to faint or lose his breakfast.

Poor guy. Must be quite the shock to find his trainer murdered. Especially after they'd had quite a row yesterday following the race where Samar and Jane Austen came in second. I frowned. Then again, what if Samar had killed Timmy? Maybe they didn't have the best relationship and that public fight had been the final straw.

"And when was that?" Detective Calle glanced up at the trainer.

Ralph turned to his team. "I suppose around six last night?" Samar and the other two nodded their agreement. "Timmy wasn't too happy about the way Jane Austen raced yesterday."

One of the grooms snorted and shook his head. "That's an understatement."

"Yeah." Samar's throat bobbed, his voice heavy with emotion. "Couldn't blame him, though. I should have done better."

Ralph, the assistant trainer, clapped Samar on the shoulder and gave him a gentle shake. "Don't be too hard on yourself, kid. That hardly seems important now." He grimaced as he glanced back at Timmy's body, which uniformed officers were currently zipping into a bag.

"Anyway, Timmy gave us instructions for the next day, when we were to wake Jane Austen up, what we were to feed her and how to exercise her. Normal stuff. He said he had to go answer to the stable owners, who are also not too happy about the loss."

Samar winced.

"Timmy said he'd see us in the morning." The assistant trainer shrugged again. "Typical stuff."

Detective Bennett narrowed her eyes. "Except, of course, for the fact that Timmy Pipe was upset with you all."

Ralph glanced at Samar and the two grooms, then turned back to the detective with a wry grin. "No, that was pretty typical too. Timmy was fairly notorious for his bad temper."

Samar's dark brows pinched together.

A panting officer jogged straight up to the tall Detective Bennett.

"Detective." The young man held a clipboard. "I've got the sign-in sheet from the security guard, with the records of who was here, and when, last night."

"And when they left?" Detective Bennett eagerly took the clipboard from the young officer, and with Calle looking over her shoulder, flipped through the sheets. I recognized the grid covered in signatures—it was just like the sign-in sheet I'd filled out before being allowed into the stable.

Bennett and Calle lifted their eyes to the jockey.

"You said your name is Samar Chopra?"

His nostrils flared, and he gave a slight nod.

Detective Bennett narrowed her piercing eyes. "Care to explain what you were doing in the stable last night around ten thirty?"

She spun the clipboard around and pointed at his signature. I leaned in close and was surprised to recognize a few other names who'd signed in after him, including Timmy Pipe, Jemma Watkins, Jack, and Cindy Watkins.

The older guy, Ralph, also studied the sheet, then looked up at Samar, frowning. "You came back here last night?" He tapped the sheet. "Looks like Timmy did too. But you didn't see him?"

Samar stared down at his riding boots and shook his head, his lips pressed tight together. "Nope. I checked on Jane Austen, then... just left. Must've missed him."

The detectives exchanged significant looks.

The young Detective Calle cleared her throat and turned to Timmy Pipe's team. "Any idea who might've wanted to hurt the victim?"

Ralph snorted. "Timmy had a long career, and more than his fair share of enemies. But the first name that comes to mind is Penny Zhang."

Behind me, Jack, who'd kept quiet this whole time, scoffed as if he disagreed.

But Ralph continued on. "She's had it out for Timmy for the last couple of years. She blamed him for the death of her horse, and even showed up yesterday outside the gates with that crowd of protesters." The older man's wrinkled brow pinched. "She'd love nothing more than to throw a wrench in all this and get the races canceled."

The grooms scoffed and shook their heads.

Ralph turned his head and spat. "Traitor."

Jack stepped forward and glared at Ralph. "If anyone's a traitor, it was Timmy Pipe."

They glared at each other, and the detectives once again exchanged looks. Oh boy. That didn't look great for Jack.

"That death was *all* Timmy's fault. I tried to warn him

that the horse wasn't fit to run, and he didn't listen." The weathered veterinarian turned to the detectives. "Timmy Pipe cared more about delivering the bottom line to the stable owners than he cared about his horses." He shook his head. "That might've made him a popular trainer with investors, but that's no way to treat your horses or your team."

Detective Bennett made a thoughtful noise, then flashed her eyes at Detective Calle. "Interesting. Thank you for your perspective."

Jack nodded, but Mim and I exchanged worried looks. I suspected that Jack had just made the suspect list. In fact, it was clear there was no love lost between Jack and Timmy Pipe, and while I liked Mim's friend, I wasn't sure myself that he was innocent.

Ralph, the assistant trainer, shrugged and stuffed his hands in his armpits. "Aside from the freak loss yesterday, we're the top team to beat. Anyone racing here has a motive to kill Timmy in an effort to sabotage us."

He had a point. So far, Samar, Jack, and Penny Zhang had all made my suspect list. But it sounded like Timmy Pipe had been in the horse racing business for decades and was rough around the edges. Who knew how many personal enemies he'd made, not to mention any professional rivals who might have killed him to up their own chances of winning.

I shuddered. In all likelihood, there'd be a murderer wandering around the races today.

6

SUGAR MAMA

Despite being exhausted and rattled by discovering a dead body, I dragged myself in to work the tearoom tent. When I told the guys about the "excitement" that morning, Fitz's concerned eyes searched my face with an intensity that made me blush, and everybody wrapped me in hugs. My vampire boss suggested I go back to the inn and rest, but I waved it off.

While I'd have loved to get more sleep, I doubted I could right now. As soon as I closed my eyes, I knew I'd see Timmy Pipe lying in the hay—cold—dead. Besides, Fitz needed my help. The second day of the races was supposed to draw an even higher attendance than the first, and he was a bit out of his comfort zone. Considering the guy was stuck in a hundreds-of-years-long rut—basically only visiting his estate, tearoom, and Gus's place—convincing him to host the marquee for the weekend hadn't been easy.

Ultimately, I'd convinced Fitz it would be worth it and be great exposure for the Bath Butler Cafe, but he'd been reluctant. And so far, he seemed more than a little out of sorts.

I shuffled about, taking orders and stifling yawns as customers poured in. I guessed about half of them were hardcore racing fans—eyes glued to the track or the televisions, cheering for every race—and about half were just here to enjoy the party atmosphere—big hats, mimosas, and all.

Among the early birds was our new regular, Gary. He sat at the same table he'd occupied all day yesterday, only now, Cindy Watkins joined him. I supposed he hadn't been fibbing about her picking up his tab.

As I bussed a nearby table, I snuck glances their way. They sat with their heads bent close together as Cindy poured Gary another steaming cup of tea. What did she see in that guy? Cindy was an attractive lady and a well-known stable owner. Her daughter, Jemma, had beaten Jane Austen in the race yesterday. Yet here Cindy was, playing hostess for frumpy Gary, who seemed all too eager to overindulge at her expense.

Cho sidled up beside me, and I jumped, realizing I'd been staring at the two.

"Sorry." Cho winced. "Didn't mean to spook you. I know you've had... a tough morning."

I snorted. Yeah, finding a dead body hadn't been the best way to start the day. "No worries. I was just lost in thought." I frowned and jerked my chin at Cindy and Gary. "I wonder how those two know each other."

He shrugged as I scooped up my tray and followed him to the back of the tent to the makeshift kitchen. "No clue, but he's racking up an *enormous* bill on her tab." He let out a wistful sigh. "Maybe I should get a sugar mama."

I shot him a flat look.

"What?" He fought a grin. "I mean if *Gary* can pull it off, surely I could."

I raised a brow. "I think you should aim higher." I knew Cho liked to joke and wasn't being serious. Besides, I doubted Cindy was Gary's "sugar mama." Their relationship seemed more professional to me—like she was wining and dining him over a business deal or something. Maybe Gary was an investor?

The low roar of the crowd and blare of television announcers faded as we entered the kitchen, where the raucous noises were replaced by the clangs of pots and pans and shouted orders between cooks and servers.

I set my dirty dishes beside the pile next to the sink, where Calvin scrubbed away in rubber gloves and an apron. Cho and I slid past the young, freckled butler over to Fitz, to pick up our tiered trays of finger foods and steaming pots of tea.

I clenched my jaw as the pretty chef giggled at something Fitz said.

My handsome vampire boss blinked at her in surprise, as though caught off guard that she found something he said amusing. "It wasn't in jest. I truly don't own a cell phone."

She tittered again. "Oh, Fitzy."

I rankled at the nickname. Fitzy? Since when was she so familiar with him? Besides, Fitzy was the sort of name you gave a yappy little dog.

She smacked his arm, and I had to turn toward the counter to keep from glaring at her.

"You're hilarious. You sure know how to make a woman work for your number. Just so you know, I didn't become a top chef and open my own restaurant by giving up easily."

Was he interested in her? Carmen was lovely and shared his talent for cooking. Besides, they were both business owners. I imagined they might actually have some things in common. I found her flirting obnoxious and over-the-top, but maybe that's what a reserved gentleman like Fitz needed. A woman who'd make the first move. My stomach twisted with angst, and I glanced at my vampire boss to gauge his reaction.

Fitz's dark eyes grew wide, and his pale skin flushed a bright pink. You knew it was real when a pale vampire blushed. He opened his mouth to reply but caught sight of us. His eyes lit up. "Minnie! Cho!"

The jealous heat that had flared up in my chest was somewhat cooled by the fact that Fitz looked so grateful to see us. The pretty chef's gaze swept over us, lingered on me for a long moment, and then she turned back to her own cooking.

Fitz's thick brows pinched in concern. "How are you feeling?" He didn't wait for me to answer. "I know my... protectiveness isn't always welcome, but please consider taking the day off."

I shot him a grateful grin, then glanced down at the pile of delicious-looking cranberry scones steaming on the tray beside me. Since Fitz had lived his formative years during the Regency and was still working on letting go and moving on from those times, he was a gentleman through and through. Which led him to be dreamily romantic, gallant, and proper.

And on the flipside, it also caused him to sometimes view me as a member of the "weaker" sex, in need of sheltering. Which, to a modern young woman like myself, grated on my nerves. We'd been working on it though, and I was grateful for Fitz reining it in a bit.

"I appreciate that, but I'm doing all right. I couldn't leave you here to fend for yourself."

Already, the normally composed and somewhat aristocratic Fitz had nearly had a meltdown when we temporarily couldn't find his favorite rolling pin. I hadn't realized how difficult it would be for him to mix up his routine, but I knew he'd only agreed to come to Derbyshire because I'd proposed it. I couldn't abandon him now.

"Besides, I think some of the shock of discovering Timmy like that has worn off." I shuddered as I imagined a murderer wandering around in our midst. "I hope the police figure out who killed him, and fast."

Fitz edged closer to me so that his arm brushed against mine. His chilled skin made me look up into his concerned face. "In the meantime, I intend to keep you safe."

I grinned, my cheeks warm, and felt better—both about the flirting chef and the murder case. Fitz had a way of making me feel seen and heard, and I knew he cared about me. Plus, I believed this hundreds-of-years-old, supernaturally strong vampire when he told me he'd protect me.

"Thank you."

A grin tugged at the edges of his lips before he shook his wavy dark hair out of his eyes and returned to rolling shortbread dough. He paused and glanced around at the floury worktop. "Zounds! Now where is my..." He sucked in air over his teeth as he ducked left and right.

"Cookie cutter?" I grinned and reached behind me for the metal circle, then handed it to him.

He groaned.

"I know change is hard, but you're doing great." I winked. "I've got your back, just like you've got mine."

He shot me a grateful smile and I grabbed the nearest tea tray, checked the receipt to make sure it was for my table, then sidled past Cho and Calvin back out into the crowded tent.

As I headed for my table, a couple of uniformed officers

entered the tent and scanned the crowd. I froze, sure for a moment that they were looking for me. But my unfounded worry turned to curiosity as they marched over to Cindy and Gary, spoke in low voices, and then escorted Cindy out of the tent.

Dom, with his absurdly wide shoulders and handsome, chiseled face stood nearby, also watching. After Cindy and the officers disappeared out of sight, he turned and flashed his eyes. "Think this has to do with Timmy Pipe's murder?"

I lowered my voice so our customers wouldn't hear. "Definitely. You said Cindy's a famous horse breeder, right?"

Dominik nodded.

"I bet the police are questioning anybody who knew the man."

Dominik snorted. "That's gonna be a long list. Timmy was a famous trainer for decades. He knew everybody in the business."

True. I lingered a moment longer before heading to serve my table. Was Cindy just one person of interest among many? Or did the police have a reason to suspect her in particular?

7

LUNCH BREAK UP

The morning flew by, with the races thundering on below, the stands full of cheering fans, and the tearoom tent bustling with customers. For hours, every table was full, and we even had a line to get in. At least this latest marketing gamble of mine was paying off for the Butler Cafe.

As I served teapots, took orders, and cleared plates, I couldn't help but overhear conversations. The whole place seemed to be buzzing with gossip about Timmy Pipe's murder. And no wonder. He was a famous trainer, and his death had rocked the races.

Between the long day on my feet and the shock of discovering Timmy's body, by the time business slowed, I was more than ready for my lunch break. I grabbed the tuna sandwich and fresh scone (chocolate chip, my favorite) that Fitz had prepared for me, then wandered off to find a quiet spot.

With all the thunderous applause and screams from the stands, and the constant hubbub of conversation in the tearoom tent, I was feeling completely zapped and in need of some peace and quiet. I had a staff pass that allowed me access to the big field that bordered the pasture where horses grazed and grooms exercised them on the other side of the white picket fence.

My shoulders relaxed, and I felt my nerves ease as I wandered through the thick grass, the sun shining on my face and a gentle breeze rustling the trees around the perimeter. It was such a beautiful setting, and I felt grateful for a moment to appreciate it. A rider galloped by on a brown horse in the distance, and a few staff gathered outside the stable, chatting, but for the most part I had the field to myself.

I ambled toward a small line of trees, then settled in with my back against a mighty trunk, my legs stretched out in front of me. I crossed my ankles and relaxed in the cool shade, happy to watch all the hubbub of the races from *far* across the field. The gentle breeze rustled the tree leaves overhead, and I let out a sigh, relieved to be off my feet and away from the chaos and crowds.

I eagerly unwrapped the sandwich Fitz had packed for me and was just about to take a huge bite when raised voices startled me.

"You can't be serious!"

I frowned and, with serious disappointment, quietly wrapped my sandwich and set it on the ground. I rolled onto my hands and knees and crawled around the side of the tree trunk, rising just high enough to peer over the bushes. My heart picked up its pace when I spotted Samar Chopra pleading with Jemma Watkins, the jockey who'd beaten him in the race yesterday.

"Please. I didn't have a choice."

What were the two rival jockeys arguing about in this

secluded corner of the pasture? With my witchy senses tingling, I held still and listened.

Jemma whirled to face Samar, her blond ponytail tied with a blue ribbon. She stood with her arms straight at her sides and her hands balled into fists. "Why would you do that?"

Samar's dark brows pinched together, his black eye looking even worse in the sunshine. He reached his hands out to the other jockey, pleading. "Jemma, your mother told me everything, okay? The money scheme? You were going to be in trouble, real trouble, unless I went along with her plan."

Jemma recoiled. "The money scheme? What are you talking about?"

I raised a brow. My thoughts exactly. Something strange was going on here. Not only was Samar fighting with the rival jockey, but it seemed like he was in cahoots with her mother, Cindy.

Jemma pursed her lips and glared at Samar. "What did my mother tell you, exactly?"

Samar looked miserable—his brows pinched and shoulders slumped. He edged closer to Jemma and reached for her hands. "I love you. I think if you didn't already know that, what I did for you proves it."

Whoa. These two were in love? Had he killed Timmy Pipe to somehow prove his love for Jemma?

Samar licked his lips. "You don't have to hide it from me anymore, I already know everything. We'll figure this out together."

The blonde made a disgusted noise and pulled her hands free from Samar's. She returned to her agitated pacing. "I think last night proves I love you too, but what are you talking about? I'm not hiding anything from you!" She threw her hands up. "You're the one going behind my back, making your little plans with my mother."

It was Samar's turn to be exasperated. He raked his hands through his dark, curly hair. "I did it for *you*, obviously." He let out a frustrated huff. "Why can't you see that?"

The young woman whirled to face him and held up her palms. "This whole thing is so messed-up." She backed away from Samar, waving her hands at him. "I need some space to think."

She whirled and marched out of the little copse of trees, across the open field, and away from the races.

"Jemma! Come back!"

Samar watched as she marched away, then hung his head and trudged back toward the stable. I ducked down below the bushes and crawled back to my place at the base of the tree trunk. I grabbed my sandwich and took a small bite, my stomach suddenly unsettled.

Money scheme? What were they talking about, and why were Samar and Jemma's mom, Cindy, working together? Samar's team and Jemma and Cindy's were rivals. Then again, Samar and Jemma had just confessed their love for each other.

I slumped lower, my back resting against the hard trunk. Exhaustion weighed more heavily on me than ever, with a whirlwind of questions swirling around in my mind. One thing was clear though: the next chance I got, I'd be sure to pass on what I'd overheard to the detectives.

Every now and then I got a witchy sense, a chill down my spine, that told me something was important to pay attention to. And I had a feeling that Samar and Jemma were somehow connected to Timmy Pipe's murder.

8

THE INN

Some of the races went late, which meant spectators were still filtering into our tent for cups of coffee, dinner, and late-night snacks. It was dark and past closing by the time Fitz, the butlers, and I finished packing up the tent for the night.

With aching feet, I walked the long dirt lane with the guys back to the local inn where we were staying.

Leo held the door for us, and we trickled into the warm, cozy old cottage. Wide stairs to the left led up to the upper stories and our hotel rooms, while straight ahead, the pub and restaurant beckoned.

Aldric rubbed his palms together, an eager smile on his face. "What do you say we grab some dinner before heading upstairs to bed?"

Calvin grinned at the big teddy bear of a guy. "By that you mean dessert?"

Al chuckled as Cho threw an arm around his shoulders, grinning. "I second that!" He lifted a long finger. "And some drinks."

Despite his almost indefatigable vampire stamina, even

our boss's eyes were a bit bloodshot and weary. "I'd like to show my appreciation for all of your hard work. First round is on me."

Leo clapped him on the shoulder, then frowned, glancing between his palm and Fitz. "Thanks... boss."

I suspected Leo had been surprised by the chill that radiated off the vampire, and probably the hardness of his shoulder. I knew firsthand that it felt like grabbing a solid hunk of rock. It would take anyone by surprise.

As we filed toward an open booth in the corner, a few other patrons, no doubt in town for the races, glanced up. Though I wore jeans and a nice sweater, Fitz and the guys were still decked out in the butler uniforms they usually wore at the cafe in Bath. I'd gotten used to the gloves and coattails, a relic from Fitz's human days and the clothing he felt most comfortable in. But no doubt half a dozen handsome young men dressed to the nines was an unusual sight, especially out here in the country.

We all slid into a semicircular booth, upholstered in dark maroon leather and illuminated by a few flickering candles in the center of the table. I squeezed in between Calvin, who looked barely old enough to order a drink, and Fitz, who was probably older than the historic inn. Leo, Aldric, and Dominik slid in on Calvin's left. As the men perused their menus, I frowned and looked around.

"Did we lose Cho somewhere?"

Dom snorted, then jerked his chin toward the bar.

I scanned the crowd until I spotted Cho with his elbows against the bar, chatting up a young woman who sat with her back to us. I grinned and shook my head. "Of course."

Aldric, his eyes glued to the dessert section of the menu, chuckled his low, rumbling laugh.

Calvin pulled his lips to the side as he scanned the dishes. "What's everybody getting tonight?"

Fitz shrugged. "I think I'll get the steak."

I opened my mouth, ready to make a joke about vampires and stakes, but held back. If it'd been just me and Fitz, sure, but none of the other guys knew about his vampire status... or the fact that I was a witch. I shot a glance at him and grinned.

Like my bestie, Gus, Fitz always pretended to eat and drink, but I knew he'd be waiting to eat his real dinner in his hotel room. Maybe that was why he was a bit quiet. He'd told me he'd brought a small stash of blood bags and kept them in the mini fridge.

I sucked in a breath. I sure hoped no one from the cleaning crew discovered that.

The waitress soon swept up to our table, a notepad in hand and an apron tied around her waist. She took our orders, including a round of pints, then bustled off to the kitchen.

"Well... fancy seeing you here." The low, sultry voice startled me and the others into looking around.

Carmen, the pretty chef who'd been flirting with Fitz all day, lounged next to the stone fireplace with a glass of red wine in her hand. I felt like groaning but somehow managed to stifle it.

She'd changed out of her white chef's jacket and now wore a curve-hugging dress with a plunging neckline. My jaw tensed, and I suddenly wished the waitress hadn't taken my menu, so I'd have somewhere else to look.

"Hello, Carmen. Are you also staying here at the inn?" Fitz shot her a polite smile.

She sauntered over, hips swaying, and heat rushed to my

cheeks. Could she be any more obvious? *We get it. You're into Fitz.* I crossed my arms tight across my chest.

The chef leaned her hip against our table, her dark eyes glittering in the candlelight. "I am. What a coincidence."

I rolled my eyes and muttered to Calvin, "Not really. It's the closest inn to the races."

Calvin raised his brows at me.

"Which room are you staying in?" Carmen trailed her fingertip in swirling lines along the polished wood table. "Maybe we're neighbors?"

I slapped my hands down on the table, rattling the cutlery. Everyone looked my way, startled.

"I'm going to grab a drink from the bar." Her over-the-top flirting was beyond annoying. I couldn't stop her from doing it—or Fitz from being too polite to shut it down—but I certainly didn't have to sit here and witness it.

Fitz shot me a puzzled look, his thick brows pinched together. "The waitress will be back shortly with our drinks."

I attempted a smile that probably looked crazed. "I know. Just feeling like double fisting it tonight. Can I get out? Please?" I couldn't take it one more second.

With my chest and neck flushed and hot, I felt suddenly trapped sitting in the middle of the booth and unable to escape from watching Carmen's aggressive advances.

Dominik slid out of the booth and rose. "You know, I could go for an extra drink too. I'll go with you, Minnie."

I gave him a grateful nod and thanked Al, Leo, and Calvin, who slid out behind him. I set my jaw, didn't even glance back to see if Carmen had taken the empty space beside Fitz, then marched to the bar. Dom trailed slightly behind me.

"You all right?"

I slid up beside Cho, who had his back to me, still chatting up the girl. I let out a heavy sigh through my nose and said flatly, "Never been better."

Dom leaned his beefy forearms against the bar beside mine and gave me a gentle nudge with his massive shoulders. "If it makes you feel any better, I don't think he's into her."

It did make me feel slightly better... and also a little worse. I winced and glanced over at him. "Am I being that obvious?" I shook my head at myself. "And here I was judging *Carmen* for being over-the-top."

I hung my head. I wasn't really upset with *her*. Fitz was single, good-looking, and made the most ridiculously delicious scones—no wonder she was interested.

Dominic let out a low, deep chuckle. "Minnie, it's obvious that you and Fitz have a connection. And it's understandable that you'd be frustrated with Carmen laying it on *so thick*."

I raised a palm. "Right? Thank you. She's being so aggressive." I glanced over my shoulder at our table, where she still perched, chatting with Fitz. "What's more annoying than anything, though, is that it seems to be working."

I gazed at the rows of bottles behind the bar, trying to puzzle it out. "Fitz is moving so slowly, and I'm trying to be respectful of that." I pressed a hand to my heart. "I mean, I'm fresh out of a divorce, I get it. But do I need to be more like Carmen? Is that what he wants?"

Dominic pressed his plump lips together. "Fitz is a gentleman and keeps a respectful distance in everything he does." He shrugged. "If you no longer like the pace of things, maybe it's time to let him know that." He shot me a little grin. "You know—get things moving along."

I slumped my shoulders. "Maybe you're right." I'd been

okay with a slower courtship, as Fitz had put it, until Carmen decided to do some courting of her own.

Cho spun around to order a drink and noticed us for the first time. "Oh, hey guys!" He took a step back and gestured at the pretty young woman to his right, and then at Dom and me. "Penny, these are my friends and coworkers, Dominik and Minnie. You guys, this is Penny."

Dom's dark eyes went wide. "You're Penny Zhang!"

9

PENNY

"You're amazing!"

I blinked in surprise—I'd never seen the reserved Dom so animated before.

The young woman, with her long, dark hair pulled back into a low ponytail, waved him off.

"No, really, when you won the Cheltenham five years ago? Insane!"

Dominik, his eyes glued to Penny, slid past me and in between her and Cho. Cho raised his palm and shook his head at Dom's back. I couldn't help but grin. Dom was a looker. Frankly, he looked like one of those models you see rising shirtless out of the water in cologne ads.

I'd seen countless girls try to get his attention and strike out. It wasn't that he was rude, he just seemed oblivious to it. I'd never once seen him show interest in a girl before now. Unfortunately, that came at Cho's expense.

"And that final jump in the 2018 trials? Epic!" Dominic rattled off Penny's many racing accomplishments. When he finally sucked in a breath, I chuckled and caught his eye.

"You're just *casually* interested in horse racing, huh?"

His cheeks flushed a little pink, and he shrugged. He'd certainly downplayed his interest the other day.

Penny took a sip of her clear, bubbly drink and waved him off. "I appreciate your enthusiasm, but that was a different time." She shook her head. "I protest the races now."

Dom sobered, and looked at her with concern, his brows pinched. "Because of what happened two years ago?"

Penny sucked on her lips and nodded.

It suddenly occurred to me that I was speaking with the jockey whose horse had been killed because her trainer, the recently murdered Timmy Pipe, had ignored Jack's advice that the horse wasn't fit to race.

My witchy senses tingled.

"I'm sorry if this is insensitive, but... what happened?" I already knew the basics, but I wanted to hear her side of it.

Penny snorted and shot me a challenging look. I took in her glossy, bloodshot eyes and the way she was slightly swaying on her barstool. She seemed tipsy—maybe she'd tell me more than she normally would have. "My horse fell on one of the last jumps in the race and broke her leg. We had to put her down." She narrowed her dark eyes. "I've dreamt of that horse every night for two years now. You think you love your dog or cat? Times that by a hundred and you *might* know how I felt about Black Lightning. We were connected in a way that most people can't understand."

My stomach tightened, and I thought of Tilda, my familiar who was snoozing upstairs in my hotel room. I knew what Penny meant by being connected to an animal like that. Tilda was my pet and my little fur baby, but she was more than that. We worked together, she amplified my powers, and could sense my moods and always helped me when I was feeling upset or scared. The thought of her getting hurt, much less losing her life, made me sick to my stomach.

I winced. "I'm so sorry. That's horrible."

Penny nodded. "It is. It's horrible that these races are continuing. The jump races especially are so dangerous. Several horses die every cup, though so far, these races seem to be luckier than usual."

I had a feeling Mim and her charms were responsible for that.

"Even more horrible is the fact that the racing division allowed Timmy Pipe to keep being a trainer. It was his fault that my horse died! He should have been kicked out, banned for life." She made a disgusted noise and shook her head, then took a swig from her glass. "Instead, he was still considered one of the best trainers in the business. Disgusting."

Cho looked from Penny to me. "Isn't he the guy you found dead this morning?"

I nodded, and Penny shot him a dark look. "Timmy Pipe got *exactly* what he deserved."

Wow. I raised my eyebrows in surprise. She certainly wasn't trying to hide her hatred for the guy. The only person who seemed to be as upset with Timmy as she was, was Mim's veterinarian friend, Jack. Penny was inching toward the top of my list of suspects. I hoped the detectives were looking into her. She certainly had a strong motive for wanting Timmy dead.

I thought back to that argument I'd witnessed between Jemma and Samar earlier in the afternoon—maybe Penny could give me a little context.

"Sorry to change the subject, but how about jockeys? I've always been curious, are there rivalries between you all?"

Penny took a sip of her drink, the ice cubes clinking

against the glass. "There are big egos, so yeah, sometimes rivalries develop." She shrugged. "But it's a small world. Most of us are friends behind the scenes."

She glanced down at the glossy wood bar. "It was tough to lose that community when I left." She glanced up and smirked. "Sometimes I still sneak into the locker room to visit with old friends. It's like a secret club. Even if you retire, like me, you never really leave. "

If the jockeys were all friendly, for the most part, then maybe Samar and Jemma being an item wasn't that big a deal. It also meant that Penny was still granted access to areas that were normally off-limits to the public.

Though I hadn't spotted her name on the security sign-in sheet, maybe she knew the guard outside the stables and was let in. And if she'd had access to the stables, then she might've had the opportunity to kill Timmy Pipe.

I turned back to the retired jockey. "You must know Samar Chopra then?"

Penny nodded. "Yeah. I haven't talked to him in a while, but he's a good kid. Very respectful, polite, and hardworking. I never heard him complain once."

I lifted a brow. "Did you hear any rumors about him and Jemma?"

She snorted and dipped her chin to level me with a disbelieving look. "Jemma Watkins? You mean, 'Mom I want-kins'?" She chuckled. "That's what we all called her behind her back. She's a spoiled brat. She never even *deigned* to muck out stalls." She lifted her index finger from her glass of what looked like whiskey. "Most of us *worked* our way up to being a jockey, but Mommy Cindy just handed it all to her daughter on a silver platter." Penny shrugged. "I mean, Samar probably has a bit of a crush on her, most of the guys did." She rolled her eyes. "She's pretty,

I guess, but I don't see them together. They're total opposites."

Based on what Penny had just said, I was having a hard time seeing them together too. And yet I'd witnessed them declaring their love for each other. So maybe Samar and Jemma being together *was* a secret. I bit my lip and made a mental note to pass along everything I'd overheard to the detectives tomorrow.

10

AN ARREST

The next morning, I headed to the track early with all the guys, Fitz, and even Tilda, who decided to tag along. It was the second-to-last day of the races, and we anticipated even more business than the previous two days. I steeled myself for long hours with aching feet and a tired mind. I needed to ask Mim if there was a spell for my feet—now that would be some practical magic.

We were barely an hour into the morning shift, all the tables full of people taking morning tea and diving into Fitz's delicious English breakfast, when a startled voice made me look up from taking an order.

"Minnie? Minnie!"

Mim, her blue eyes wide and wild, darted between the tables and rushed up to me. I excused myself from my customers and waved Leo down to take over for me.

I pulled Mim aside. "Are you alright?" Normally, the older witch was unflappable and always had an air of mystery, as if she knew something I didn't. I'd never seen her startled, much less panicked before.

She gripped my shoulders in both her hands and shook her head, her throat bobbing as she tried to catch her breath. "Those dolts of police! They arrested Jack!"

I glanced to my left at several nearby tables. Patrons glanced up, startled at her words, so I guided Mim a little farther away. Cindy Watkins sat at a table with Gary, who was already three mimosas in, and leaned our way, eavesdropping.

I lowered my voice so we wouldn't be overheard and gave Mim a steady gaze. "Really? They arrested Jack?" A twinge of guilt tugged at my stomach, since I'd somewhat suspected him too.

Her eyes welled with tears as she fought to catch her breath. "Jack and I were in the stables this morning, like usual, doing... you know."

I was happy to know that they'd carried on their work checking and charming the horses.

Mim sucked in a breath and continued. "Then the police showed up, those two detectives, and they hauled Jack away for Timmy Pipe's murder!"

Jack might've been rightfully angry with Timmy Pipe for going against his recommendations and ultimately getting a horse killed. But Jack didn't seem like a murderer. Then again, all the murderers I had met never actually *seemed* like killers.

But if it had been Jack, why now? That accident happened two years ago. It just didn't make sense.

"Did the police say why they were arresting him?"

Mim scowled. "I guess quite a few witnesses testified to Jack and Timmy having a long-standing hate for each other. And Jack apparently was signed into the stable around the time of death. No one was with him, so they can't confirm he *didn't* kill that man."

I frowned. "Is that all?" That seemed like pretty weak, circumstantial evidence.

Mim rolled her eyes skyward toward the peak of the tent. "Well… that and apparently they found the murder weapon. It was a shovel they found in the stable, and it had not only Timmy's blood on it, but Jack's fingerprints, as well." She flashed her eyes at me. "Well, duh! Sometimes Jack has to shovel some droppings out of the way so we can check on the horses." She threw her hands up. "The cursed thing probably has a dozen grooms' prints on it too. But Jack's the only one with a motive and no alibi, so they're bringing him in to the station."

I looked over her head toward the entrance to the tent, where a short queue already formed. "When did this happen?"

Mim panted. "Just now." She pressed her hand against her side. "I ran over here straight away to tell you. You always seem to get to the bottom of things." She whimpered and cast about desperately. "I thought maybe you'd know what to do."

I caught her eye. "I overheard something yesterday, between Samar and Jemma—apparently they're more than just friends, and I think they're up to something. If I can speak to the police, it might get your friend off the hook."

A fork clattered on a plate, and Mim and I glanced over. We caught Cindy Watkins staring at us. Her eyes widened, and she quickly looked down at her plate.

Shoot. Samar and Jemma had argued about Cindy—had she been involved? My stomach twisted with unease. She probably wasn't too pleased to overhear that I was about to tell the detectives about her daughter and the rival jockey, Samar, being possibly connected to Timmy Pipe's murder.

Oh well. She'd just have to suck it up.

Mim nodded, her eyes frantic. “Let’s hurry!”

By the time Mim and I spotted the detectives and Jack, we were completely out of breath, and they were halfway down the lane back to the inn.

“Wait!”

When the two detectives, the two uniformed officers, and Jack whirled around, Mim waved her arms high overhead, panting.

I sucked in a breath, sweat beading at my hairline. “Wait! I have some information!”

The two detectives exchanged looks, muttered a few words between them, and then Detective Bennett planted a hand on her hip. “Alright, let’s have it.” She beckoned us forward, and Mim and I staggered down the lane. Sweat tickled my neck, and Mim clutched a stitch in her side.

Jack’s concerned gaze darted between the two of us. “I’m no happier about this than you are, ladies, let me tell you. But I don’t want you two getting mixed up in anything.”

Mim continued to pant heavily and waved him off. “Oh, have off it. We get mixed up in everything.”

This got a grin out of Jack.

Detective Bennett raised a dark brow at me. “Ms. Wells, correct?”

I nodded, still fighting to catch my breath.

She gave me a stern look. “We’re quite busy. This information?”

I sucked in a heaving breath. “Jack didn’t do it. You should look into Samar Chopra and Jemma Watkins.” My chest ached with the effort of chasing the officers down. “They’re romantically involved.”

Detective Bennett frowned at me, and then she and her partner exchanged significant looks.

"What?" Mim folded forward, her hands on the thighs of her long skirt.

Detective Bennett crossed her arms and looked me up and down. "Cindy Watkins called me, just now, and told me that she'd forgotten to mention something. Apparently, her daughter Jemma and Samar got engaged recently. The night our victim was murdered, to be precise. They all celebrated together that night—apparently Jemma couldn't wait to share the good news with her mother."

I scoffed. "And they all just *forgot* to tell you that?"

Detective Bennet stayed stoic, but the tiniest lift of her brow hinted to me that she agreed it was suspicious.

"She was in the tent." I shot an incredulous look at Mim, then turned back to the detectives. "We were discussing coming to find you, and Cindy must've overheard me saying I was going to tell you about Jemma and Samar." I shook my head, disgusted. "She called you to get ahead of the situation."

I had to give it to Cindy, she was sneaky. And it made me suspect all the more that she, Samar, and Jemma were up to something.

I hurried to explain to the detectives, while I had their attention.

"I overheard an argument between Jemma and Samar yesterday afternoon." I shook my head. "It didn't sound like they were talking about an engagement. Samar mentioned some secret, something that was going on between him and Cindy behind Jemma's back."

Mim nodded, her wiry gray hair bouncing over her shoulders. "Besides, why wouldn't Cindy have told you about the engagement before? Seems that would give them all an alibi for the night of Timmy Pipe's murder."

Detective Bennett sucked in a deep breath through her nose and gave the two of us hard looks. "Apparently, they wanted to keep it a secret. Cindy claims *she* was supportive of the union, but they feared the other breeder, who owns Jane Austen, might think it'd interfere with Samar's ability to compete against his fiancée. Especially given his loss to her the day before."

Mim and I exchanged doubtful looks. That sort of made sense... but something still felt off to me.

"This timing—just seems strange."

Detective Bennett shrugged. "We've got a trainer bashed in the head, twice, with a horse shovel. Tell me what's not strange."

She had a point. "Wait—he was hit twice?"

Bennett studied me a moment, then nodded. "Two blows. One to the front of the head, and another to the back of it." She narrowed her eyes at Jack. "Someone wanted to make sure our victim was dead." She sighed and jerked her head. "Let's go."

They started to move on, but Jack leaned back, slowing the officers at his elbows down. He pleaded with Mim and me, "Please... find a way to keep those horses safe."

Mim nodded, her eyes welling with tears. I bit my lip—even as he was getting arrested, this man was thinking of those beautiful animals. I just couldn't see him committing a cold-blooded murder.

After the officers escorted Jack out of sight, Mim turned to me, sniffling. "I'd better get back to the races." She swiped tears off her cheeks. "Do my best to spell the horses safe from the stands." She whimpered. "Oh, but it's going to be so much harder to keep track of all of them and keep them from getting hurt."

I pressed my lips together and took her hands in mine. "Do your best, and I'll help when I can."

Her bright blue eyes searched my face, her brows pinched together. "Minnie... while I do that, will you do your best to clear Jack's name?"

I opened my mouth to protest that I wasn't sure how to do that, when she stepped closer and cut me off.

"Please, Minnie!" She squeezed my hands. "You've solved murders before. Please, look into this. Maybe start with Samar and Jemma? I think you're onto something there."

I hesitated. I had my plate full working at the tearoom tent, and though she was correct that I had solved a few murders, I was no trained detective. Plus, I'd almost gotten myself killed in the process. Still, Mim was begging for my help. She was a powerful witch and had become a good friend and mentor.

I swallowed and gently squeezed her hands. "I'll do my best to clear Jack's name and find the real killer. I can't promise anything, but... I'll try."

Mim's face crumpled, and she threw her arms around me in a tight hug, smushing me against her beaded blouse and enveloping me in a cloud of patchouli and lavender.

"Oh, thank you!"

I hugged her back—and hoped I'd be able to deliver.

11

CAT GOT YOUR TONGUE

There were few people whose opinions I trusted more than Fitz's. After Mim and I hurried back to the races and she disappeared into the stands to cast spells over the horses, I sought out my vampire boss. I needed to get back to serving tables with the butlers, but first I slid through the bustling tent, between round tables littered with teacups and trays, and into the kitchen area in the back.

Steam rose from pots on the stove, and Calvin nodded hello as he scrubbed dishes. I gave him a tight grin, then sidled up to Fitz, who sliced the crusts off some cucumber sandwiches. He stopped what he was doing and shot me a concerned look, a stray lock of dark, wavy hair hanging over his eyebrow.

"What's happened?" He glanced behind me, eyes blazing, as if looking for the person who'd put me in such a worried state.

I slid close to him so we wouldn't be overheard and was momentarily distracted by the cold radiating off him, carrying the scents of rosemary and fresh-baked bread. I composed myself and filled him in. "They've arrested Jack, Mim's veterinarian friend, for Timmy Pipe's murder."

Fitz frowned. "And you don't think he did it?"

I shook my head and opened my mouth to explain about Samar and Jemma, when Carmen, the pretty chef, sidled up between us.

"Sorry, am I interrupting something?" She batted her dark eyes at Fitz, completely ignoring me.

"Actually, we were—"

She cut me off, beaming a charming smile at my boss. "Because Fitz, I needed to ask you a question about something. Is this sauce better with or without the garlic?" She held up a spoon and moved it toward Fitz's mouth to taste.

Lucky for her, the whole garlic-repels-vampires thing was a myth. I wished it could repel overly flirtatious chefs, though. A wave of jealous heat flushed across my chest.

Fitz frowned down at the spoon she lifted closer to his lips, then leaned back. "Apologies, but Minnie and I were discussing something rather urgent."

Carmen waved it off. "Oh, of course!" She winked at Fitz. "I don't mind waiting."

I huffed, thoroughly annoyed. Trying to talk this out with Fitz was clearly going to be a dead end at the moment. I set my jaw. "It's fine." I shrugged at my boss. "I'll talk to you later."

Though Fitz looked like he wanted to say more, I spun on my heel to go—not quite sure *where* I was going.

Tilda leapt out from her hiding spot under one of the long tablecloths as I stomped across the tent and trotted along beside me. I shot her a grateful grin. "Hey, girl." Then I shot Leo an apologetic look as I walked back out of the tent. The guys were swamped and could use my help, but I needed a minute to sort my thoughts.

I ducked out of the tent and stalked off toward the pasture, with Tilda jogging beside me, until I found a relatively quiet spot in a shaded passageway and pulled out my phone. If Fitz was too busy to discuss the case with me, I'd have no choice but to try my bestie, Gus.

I groaned as his phone went to voicemail and mentally face palmed myself—it was morning. Which meant my nocturnal friend would be sleeping.

I hung up without leaving a message and shoved my phone back into my pocket. "Guess I'll just have to figure out this murder case and clear Jack's name on my own, then. No biggie." I let out a heavy sigh.

I think it was the blond woman.

I gasped and looked around, but no one stood nearby or seemed to pay me any attention. I was in the shade under a mossy stone archway, distanced from the rest of the noisy hustle and bustle. So where had that voice come from? It'd sounded like a woman had been standing right beside me....

I blew out a shaky breath. Now I was hearing things. "Too many late nights." Unless... I grinned. "Is this that inner voice Mim keeps telling me to listen to?"

No. It's me, you little dum-dum.

The sweet, singsong female voice startled me all over again. With my heart racing, I pushed my back against the cool stone wall and looked around. I had a sneaking suspicion I knew who the voice belonged to, but if I was right... did it make me crazy?

Holding my breath, I dropped my gaze—just my eyes at first, and then dipped my chin. Tilda sat in front of me, her tail curled around her front paws, eyes bright and expectant —as if waiting for me to respond.

I gulped and whispered, "Tilda?"

Dur!

She didn't move—not even a whisker twitched. But somehow, she'd spoken to me, her voice loud inside my head.

"Holy cow." I dragged my hands through my hair and gaped at her. "Holy cow!"

My familiar cleaned herself. *Eh. I like their eyelashes, but I don't know what's so holy about them. They smell yucky.*

I crouched down in front of her. I looked around to make sure we were still alone, then stared into Tilda's bright yellow eyes.

"Can I hear you because of that spell I cast at the standing stones at the Solstice?"

Her ears swiveled toward me. *Me no know.*

I grinned, a giddy rush shooting through me. "It has to be the spell. That means it's working! My powers are growing stronger—and our connection is blooming." I gawked. "This is so cool!"

Yes. Tilda nodded, her voice high and innocent in my head. *It's a good thing too.* She lifted her paw and softly placed it on the back of my hand. *Because you need my help, you dumb witch.*

I pressed my lips together. She said it so sweetly and cheerfully, it was hard to take offense, and yet my cat clearly thought she was superior to me. I raised a brow. I guess that made her like every other cat on the planet.

I shifted my weight and flipped my hand so that her soft black paw rested in my palm. So cute. I rubbed the back of her mitt with my thumb, and she snatched it back, scrunching her nose.

No. Don't like.

I nodded. "Sorry." I cleared my throat, glanced around again, and then lowered my voice. "So, when you say I need your help... did you mean with the murder case?"

She tilted her head. *I meant with everything, but sure.*

We'd just push right past that one. "So... when you said you thought the blond lady did it...?"

The tip of her tail flicked. *The lady at the table with the large man. She wouldn't pet me.*

Did she mean Cindy? I chuckled. "Is that your only reason for suspecting her? Maybe she just has allergies or didn't want to get her hands dirty while eating finger food."

Tilda's yellow eyes narrowed to slits. *What are you implying? I'm very clean.*

Touchy. I waved it off. "I just meant, do you have any other evidence?"

Tilda stood, stretched, and then nuzzled her cheek against my knee. I guessed I was forgiven.

Just my instincts. That's all I need.

"Fair enough, but humor me? Let's go through the suspects. Besides, even if it was Cindy, we're going to need some hard evidence, not just instincts, to prove it to the police and get Jack off the hook."

Tilda squeezed her eyes shut as she continued to rub her face on my knee. *Jack sounds good. He's nice to animals, right?*

I nodded and had to agree with her there. It was hard for me to imagine anyone who was kind to animals being a killer... unless they killed to defend animals.

I blew out a breath and started on the list, as much to bounce it off Tilda as to help organize the suspects in my own mind. If I couldn't discuss the case with Fitz or Gus, I had to admit, my cute little familiar made a great alternative.

"Okay, so we've got Timmy Pipe, this infamous trainer, killed in the stables."

I paused as a jockey walked by and shot me and Tilda a grin. I smiled back, waited for him to pass, then jumped back in.

"Penny Zhang had a motive—revenge for Timmy's decision that resulted in her horse's death. She also could've gotten access to the stable, since she said she still gets preferential treatment around here."

Tilda flopped down onto her side, her head lifted and tail tapping the dirt. I ran my hand down her back, and she laid her head contentedly down.

"I hate to admit it, but we can't entirely cross Jack off the list, either. The veterinarian was also angry with Timmy over that horse's death. I don't think he did it, but we have to examine all angles."

Tilda sniffed. *Oh, silly billy, just trust your gut. He didn't do it.*

I grinned. "I'll take it under consideration." I swallowed as I cast through my memory to my picnic lunch the day before. "Then there's Samar and Jemma. Timmy was Samar's trainer, and he was super angry at Samar for losing the race yesterday—maybe Samar just got sick of it and lashed out?"

Tilda purred as I petted her back. *Maybe.*

"Penny said Samar was kind of a quiet, gentle guy. Which is odd, considering he's engaged to Jemma, who's rumored to be a bit bratty and entitled." I scrunched up my face. "But, if the girl won't muck stalls, is she really going to get her hands dirty and murder someone?"

No.

I bit my lip. "She could've gotten Samar to kill Timmy for her." I narrowed my eyes. "But what's her motive? From the way she and Samar were arguing, it sounded like there was more to the story. She said something about how Samar can't really be going through with it—with *what*?"

Beats me. Tilda pawed at my hand to keep me petting her.

"Plus, Samar said something about Jemma's mom, Cindy, being in on whatever the secret is."

As Tilda supervised my petting, she purred. *Yep. It was her.*

I smirked at her. "She can't be convicted on the grounds of not being a fan of cats."

Tilda raised her brows as if agreeing to disagree.

"Cindy Watkins is a famous breeder and Jemma's mom, and Timmy worked for a rival breeder. That pits them against each other, to some extent, sure. But Timmy's team lost the race the other day. What motive would Cindy have to kill him?"

I don't know. Witches be crazy.

I adjusted my crouch. "Then again, Cindy has that weird thing going on with Gary, *and* she called the detective after eavesdropping on me and Mim." I huffed. I was getting a headache trying to puzzle this all out.

"I saw Samar, Cindy, Jemma, Jack, and Timmy's names all on the security sign-in sheet, so that doesn't help us narrow it down any." Tilda batted at my shoelaces as I nibbled my lip. "How to get more information...?"

Tilda blinked up at me. *The large man seems gullible. I just had to put my paws on his chair and he fed me some of his scone.*

I tsked. "Tilda! Those aren't good for you."

Her ears pricked. *They're not good for you, either, silly goose. And you eat them like they're catnip.*

She had me there. I thought about her suggestion. "You know, you have a point." I grinned. "Gary's already a few mimosas in. Maybe if I ply him with more drinks, I can get him to share what he knows about Cindy."

Tilda blinked at me. *Good plan.*

I grinned back at her. "Thanks, Tilda."

12

MIMOSA MAGIC

I scooped Tilda into my arms and headed for the stands, where I scanned the crowd for Mim. I had an idea for a spell I wanted to ask her about, but the seats were packed, and I couldn't spot her. After a few minutes of getting jostled in the aisle, I gave up and headed back to the tent.

It'd been several months of lessons with Mim now, plus I'd been practicing on my own. Looked like I'd be improvising this spell by myself—my first time flying solo. Well, with Tilda's help, of course.

I glanced at Gary's table as I headed back to the kitchen. Cindy had left him by himself, and he was sipping tea, his eyes glued to the enormous television projecting the latest race. I gulped, buzzing with nerves, as I slid into the narrow kitchen space between tents, careful to turn in a way that kept Tilda out of view. Carmen worked with her back to Fitz but glanced over her shoulder and chuckled at something he said.

Humph.

I gently set Tilda down, hiding her under the overhang

of the worktop. The health inspectors probably wouldn't appreciate Tilda being in the kitchen—and Fitz definitely wouldn't—but this was an emergency. I yanked the huge fridge we shared with Carmen's team open and pulled out an already opened bottle of champagne from the door, along with the jug of fresh-squeezed orange juice. I tucked those under my arm, then spun around and plucked up a glass flute from beside the sink. Calvin glanced up from washing dishes briefly, and I grinned hello, then moved down the counter away from him. Although the cramped space swarmed with waiters from Carmen's restaurant, I'd somehow need to carve out a little privacy to work my magic.

Meow.

I held a finger to my lips, urging her to be quiet, then grinned down at Tilda nuzzling my leg. Not only was her furry little self comforting, but she also amplified my powers. And I could use all the help I could get.

I blew out a shaky breath and filled the champagne flute almost to the top, then added a tiny splash of orange juice. Just the way Gary liked. The alcohol itself would probably help get him to share with me, but I planned to add a little extra oomph, just to be sure.

I'd never cast a spell like this one before, but Mim always told me I just needed to concentrate on the outcome, channel my power, and find some way to focus it. When we divined, we often used a basin of water. As a water witch, that worked better for me than a crystal ball or mirror, but they served the same purpose.

I gazed down at the fizzing bubbles. Champagne and orange juice had to have some water in them—this was my medium. I could do this. I didn't have a wand or another way of focusing my magic, so I decided to use a spoken spell. I blew out a shaky breath, trying out a few different lines in my head, before settling on a simple rhyme.

I glanced to each side—Fitz, Carmen, and Calvin were all absorbed in their work, and none of the other butlers were back here. Carmen's waiters all gathered at the opposite end of the narrow space. Now was my chance.

I held my hands over the mimosa and rooted into the earth, feeling the ground beneath my feet and Tilda's warmth against my ankles. I closed my eyes and whispered,

"Bubbly, bubbly, little sips,
Work your magic to loosen lips."

My palms grew hot, and I opened my eyes as a purple flash lit up the champagne flute, then faded away. I glanced around, heart racing, but luckily no one seemed to have noticed. With champagne flute in hand, I hustled back out to the dining area of the tent and intercepted Leo on his way to Gary's table with a pitcher of water. Tilda trotted along at my heels.

"Hey!"

Leo blinked at me in surprise.

I flashed a toothy smile. "Could I take over Gary's table?"

He snorted and looked down his nose at me. "You really want to? I've been avoiding going back over to check on him. Every time I do, I have to hear all about what a VIP he is." He rolled his eyes.

I smirked. Gary was in a chatty mood already—perfect. I nodded and took the water pitcher from Leo. "Yep, I'm sure."

He shot me a quizzical look. "You know it's busy but

we've got this. You could probably take the day off and enjoy the races."

I looked around, then whispered, "I want to ask him some questions about Cindy Watkins. I think she might be involved in Timmy Pipe's murder."

"Ah." Leo gave me a slow nod and wink, bent to scratch Tilda's head, then moved off to help another table.

I bustled up to Gary with Tilda at my ankles and plastered on a bright smile. "Good morning." Ice cubes plunked into his water glass as I refilled it, and he blinked up at me, already a little bleary eyed.

"Morning."

I set down the bespelled mimosa and plucked up his empty champagne flute, a tiny puddle of orange juice in the bottom. "I thought you looked ready for another drink."

"Oh—oh, why thank you, yes I was, in fact." Gary chortled and plucked up the mimosa. I willed myself to glance up at the races on the television screen so as to avoid watching him like a hawk.

I shot him a side-eye look as he gulped the liquid down, then lowered the glass and smacked his lips. I felt a little guilty spelling him like this, but it was for a good cause. A murderer was on the loose, and I doubted the police had the real culprit.

"Mm." He held the glass up and peered at the fizzy contents. "Did you do something different? This one seems to have a little extra punch."

I grinned and slid into the empty seat next to him, where Cindy had been earlier. He raised a thick brow, but I winked in an attempt to be charming and put him at ease. As Tilda snaked between my ankles, I couldn't help but think about the comments she'd have for me later about my lack of smoothness.

"So, Gary, are you enjoying the races so far?" I crossed my fingers under the table that my spell would work.

He nodded, his double chin nearly dipping down to the cloth napkin tucked into his collar. "I am indeed!" He leaned closer, a little extra glassiness to his eyes. "Have I mentioned that I'm the *special* guest of Cindy Watkins, the famous horse breeder?"

He had—about a thousand times to anyone that'd listen. But this was the perfect segue. I beamed at him and leaned closer. "You don't say! Funny you should mention Cindy, I was wondering if—"

He held up a thick hand and cut me off. "You know, I was actually born in a small village north of here. Northeast, to be precise. It was a cold winter. My mother always said labor with me was like giving birth to a bowling ball. When I was five..."

Half an hour later, I sat slumped with my elbow on the table and my cheek in my hand. My spell to loosen Gary's lips had worked—a little too well. The phrase "be careful what you wish for" came to mind. Gary was now certainly in the sharing mood, but I was getting his entire life story—in excruciatingly boring detail. And we were only up to primary school.

Leo passed by with a tray of finger sandwiches and macarons, and he chuckled as I caught his eye and silently begged him for help. But he had tables to serve—I'd have to rescue myself.

"I actually came in third in the spelling bee that year. I lost to a boy named Quincy... or was it Quentin?"

I slapped my hand down on the table—harder than I'd meant to—and startled Gary and the tables around us.

I winced and shot apologetic looks at everyone, then

turned back to Gary before he could start up with his life story again. "So Gary, what do you do for work?"

"Oh, uh...." He blinked and shook himself. "Why, I'm an auditor. Been one for thirty years. It involves lots of spreadsheets, calculations—"

Oh no, I couldn't take it anymore. I might die of boredom. "Do you audit for the racetrack or...?"

"Oh no." Gary opened his mouth as if to say more but stopped himself.

I blinked in surprise. Since when did Gary hold his tongue? I tried pressing him in a different way.

"How do you and Cindy know each other?"

Gary looked down and scratched the back of his neck. "Er... I really shouldn't say...."

I bit my lip. *Come on potion—work your magic!*

As if it was being forced out of him, Gary grunted and gushed, "But... just between us..."

I nodded, encouraging him to keep going. *Spill it, Gary!*

"Her boss at Halliwell Construction hired me." He leaned back and covered his mouth, eyes wide.

I frowned. "Her boss? But I thought she owned her own stables?"

He sipped from the mimosa and nodded. "She does, she does. But..." He glanced around and lowered his voice. "I really shouldn't say, but she has a day job as an—*hiccup*—office manager at Halliwell Construction. Ooh." He frowned and shook his head. "Boy. I *really* shouldn't be telling you this."

I opened my mouth to question him further but froze as I spotted Cindy Watkins herself sweep into the tent. Her eyes landed on Gary—then narrowed as she spotted me speaking with him. *Eep*. Guess she was miffed about that whole tattling to the police about her daughter and Samar being together thing.

I gulped and patted the table. "Well... I better get back to work."

Bleary-eyed, Gary blinked up at me as I rose and collected the now-empty mimosa flute and crumb-covered plate beside him. I gave Cindy a polite nod as she strode up to the table.

"There you are, Gary."

He jumped and spun around in his seat. "Oh! Ms. Watkins!" He pressed a pudgy hand to his heart as if she'd nearly given him a heart attack.

She shot him a smile that didn't reach her eyes. "I've told you, call me Cindy. Let's go for that tour I mentioned, hm?" She squinted at me. "Please keep my tab open."

I nodded and waited as Gary rose, pulled the napkin from his collar, and then followed Cindy out of the tent. As I bussed the dirty dishes, with Tilda still lounging beneath one of the chairs, I mulled over what Gary had said.

All he'd told me was that Cindy had a day job at a construction firm—and that her boss had hired Gary, an auditor.

I bit my lip as I stacked plates.

Why was that such a big secret?

13

RUMORS

I got back to work, helping the butlers serve and bus tables. With business hopping and the races drawing our biggest crowds yet, Gary and Timmy Pipe's murder soon faded from my mind in all the hubbub. At the height of the lunch rush, Mim dashed in and flagged me down.

She got a few sour looks from those waiting their turn in line, but she ignored them and put a hand on my arm, breathless. "Doll, could you get me something to drink? I'm parched."

I nodded. "Of course. Should I find you somewhere to sit?" We were swamped, but I could probably find a chair for her somewhere.

She shook her head. "No time."

I frowned as I looked a little closer at my friend and mentor. Her skin was sallow, and dark bags hung under her bloodshot eyes. Her shoulders slumped below her crocheted shawl, and her breath seemed labored. "Are you alright?"

She gulped and waved me off. "I'm drained. It takes a lot

of magic to keep those horses safe, plus a lot of concentration. Constant vigilance, you know? Never know when one of them's going to take a jump wrong and stumble—or worse."

My stomach tightened, and I lowered my voice. "You're doing wonderful work, keeping those horses safe but... are you safe? I don't want you to overwork yourself." I didn't know how old Mim was exactly, but she was no spring chicken.

Mim managed a wink, despite her weary state. "Don't you worry about me." She patted my shoulder. "I've survived much worse."

Something about her tone made me think she'd seen a few things in her day. I suddenly realized that despite all the time we'd spent together during lessons, I didn't know much about Mim's past.

She interrupted my musings, her blue eyes wide and hopeful. "What have you found out?"

I knew she was hoping I'd be able to clear Jack's name soon, and I wished I had more promising news for her. "I have a few leads." I bit my lip. "Any chance the police have released Jack?"

She rolled her eyes. "No! The fools. He did call me though, from the station." She leaned close. "Apparently, a security guard confessed that he let Penny Zhang into the stable with another jockey. The guard recognized her, but she signed in under a false name."

I raised my brows. "Suspicious. So why is Jack still in custody?"

Mim planted her hands on her hips and glared. "Because the cops are grasping at straws to solve this case and desperate to close it. Penny claimed she saw Jack slinking around with a shovel in his hands."

I grimaced. "The murder weapon."

Mim flattened her lips together and nodded. "Convenient that she just happened to remember that little fact once they brought her in for questioning." She huffed. "Jack says they already released her."

I frowned, thinking it over. "What *was* Jack doing there?" I cocked my head. "And come to think of it, what was Penny doing there?"

She shook her head, her tightly coiled curls bouncing. "Jack says he made one last round to check on the horses and then went home for the rest of the night. He says he never even picked up a shovel." She stomped her foot. "Ooh! I could just hex that Penny Zhang for making up that lie."

I glanced behind Mim toward the entrance, conscious of the impatient queue of diners waiting to get a table. The line shifted on their feet and huffed. If I didn't hurry, we'd have a hungry mob in giant feathered hats on our hands. "Why would Penny make that up?"

Mim threw her hands up. "No idea! Jack hasn't a clue, either; they've always been friendly."

I blew out a heavy breath. "That's strange." Unless Jack was lying. I could tell Mim had feelings for the handsome vet—was she letting that cloud her judgement? I needed to talk to Penny to find out what she really saw.

Mim placed a hand on my arm and raised her brows. "Sorry, poppet, but could I get that drink? I'm parched." She held up a finger. "Water, please." She grinned. "And a whisky couldn't hurt."

I grinned. "Best I can do is some champagne."

She frowned but shrugged. "It'll do."

I took a step toward the kitchen to grab her drinks, but hesitated. "I could try to take over for you? You know, so you can rest for a bit?"

Mim shot me a weary, grateful smile. "Thank you, poppet, but I'm not sure you're quite ready."

Oh. My stomach fell a bit. I'd just performed an ad hoc spell that worked—maybe a little too well—on Gary. But she was probably right. Protecting those horses seemed like advanced spell casting.

She waved a hand at me. "You'll get there, doll, you will. Just not quite yet."

I gave her a little smile, then hustled back to the kitchen to round up Mim's water and champagne. Frustration burned in my chest. I hadn't known I was a witch until I came to Bath during college. Other witches I'd met, like Mim, had been practicing magic since they could walk. I felt so behind sometimes, and now I felt so helpless.

I moved into the narrow kitchen and blew out a sigh as I poured Mim a flute of champagne. The best way I could help Mim—and the horses—would be to clear Jack's name.

Unless Jack was the killer.

If only I could see what had happened that night. I sucked in a breath with excitement as a thought came to me. Maybe I didn't need the tapes to see what happened that night.

While I might not be ready to enchant racehorses, Mim had told me I was a natural at scrying. Maybe I could look into the past and figure out who killed Timmy Pipe. I'd just need a basin of water or...

I glanced around the worktop and spied a half-finished cup of tea waiting among the pile of dishes to be washed. While Calvin was busy drying, I snatched the cup up, along with Mim's champagne, and hurried back out into the tent.

Who needed a crystal ball when you had a perfectly fine cup of tea?

14

A VISION IN A TEACUP

After delivering Mim's drinks, which she carried with her back to the stands, I strode out of the tent with the teacup in hand and Tilda in tow. Leo raised a brow at me as I passed, but I just plastered on a smile and slid by the line of diners. I hated leaving the guys on such a busy day, but it wasn't like I could practice my divining in public. Besides, Leo had assured me they had it under control.

I bent my steps toward the pasture and the little copse of trees where I'd taken my lunch the previous day. The same spot where I'd overheard that argument between Samar and Jemma.

Silly. Your tea will be cold by the time you drink it.

I grinned down at Tilda, who trotted along beside me. I'd flashed my staff pass at the guys guarding the entrance to the pasture. They'd nodded at me, then done double takes when they noticed Tilda jogging along beside me. I was well on my way to earning a reputation as a crazy cat lady.

She lifted her little black nose in the air as we strode

through the lush grass, past the stables—which still gave me the willies after discovering Timmy Pipe's body in there.

"I'm not going to drink the tea, Tilda. I'm going to divine with it."

Oh. That's actually quite smart.

I shot her a look. Why did she sound so surprised?

We crossed the field and settled under the same big tree where I'd taken my lunch the day before. The branches overhead swayed gently in the breeze, and I took a few deep breaths to ground myself. Tilda curled up next to me and snuggled against my side, her soft form warm and comforting. As I felt the buzz from the races subside and began to notice the soft chirping of birds and the cool breeze against my bare arms, I knew I was ready.

I held my hands over the teacup and closed my eyes, while Tilda purred, a low rumble against my side. I tapped into her energy and the hum of nature around me, then summoned my own—the beating of my heart, the tingle in my palms, the breath against my nostrils.

I murmured a spell.

"Cup of tea,
Let me see,
What happened that night,
To Timmy Pipe."

Warmth filled my palms, and I opened my eyes. Tilda and I leaned forward and peered into the cup.

Though the tea had long since cooled, magical mist pooled on the surface, then cleared. I squinted as indistinct shapes formed. If I didn't know it was magic, I might have thought they were just shadows from the dappled light of the tree overhead. But as my familiar and I looked on, the shapes took form and played out, as if watching a miniature movie in a teacup.

I held my breath—had it worked? Were we about to see Timmy Pipe's murder? I briefly considered covering Tilda's eyes.

Fluorescent lights. Linoleum. Benches, lockers, scales, and saddles. Jockeys hurrying about.

I raised my brows. This looked like the jockeys' locker room.

A secluded area. A man's hand reached into a sort of small blanket with pockets sewn into it and added several thin, oval-shaped metal plates, about the size of mouse pads, to the pockets.

Tilda and I bent further forward over the teacup, so that her long whiskers tickled my cheek. I couldn't see the man's face, but he wore riding boots and a jersey—he had to be a jockey!

The surface of the tea rippled, and the vision faded, reflecting only the leaves and branches overhead. I blew out a breath and leaned back, as Tilda looked expectantly up at me.

Well?

I shrugged. "That was... confusing. I asked to see what happened to Timmy Pipe, and we didn't see him at all."

Tilda curled her tail around her paws. *Maybe what we saw is related to what happened to him.*

I nodded. "Probably. But I'm still confused." I scrunched up my nose, replaying the vision in my head. "What were those metal plates?" I froze as the words jogged another memory. "The detective said Timmy Pipe was killed by something metal, flat, and slightly curved—exactly like the plates we saw in the vision!"

Tilda blinked her big yellow eyes at me and placed a paw gently on my leg. *Silly. But they already found the murder weapon, right?*

"Oh yeah." I slumped. "The shovel."

I scratched Tilda's head between her ears, and she pushed into my fingers. Then I shoved to my feet, dumped out the tea, and started back across the field toward the racetrack.

Tilda trotted along beside me. *Where are we going now?*

"To speak with Penny Zhang. Mim told me that Penny gave the police a statement, claiming she saw Jack lurking around the stables the night Timmy was killed."

Do you believe her?

I shrugged at my cat. "I don't know. But if she's telling the truth, I need to find out what she saw, exactly. And if she's lying, as Jack claims, then I think we've got a good reason to slide her to the top of our suspect list. Plus, maybe she can tell me what those plates in the vision were."

15

PROTESTORS

Though Tilda and I had to fight against the stream of incoming racing patrons, once we made it outside the front gate, it wasn't difficult to locate Penny Zhang. She leaned over a police barricade, megaphone to her mouth, leading a chant for her dozens of fellow protestors.

"Rac-ing is mur-der! Rac-ing is mur-der!"

A few women in enormous hats shot her side-eye looks and hurried past. Men and women at Penny's side pumped handmade signs, featuring phrases like "Horse Racing Is *Lame*" and "Equality For Equines". Though most of them looked ready for a day at the pool, wearing sunhats and zinc stripes on their noses, I wasn't about to risk ending up on the wrong side of their zealousness.

I tucked my staff pass lanyard under my shirt—so I wouldn't be associated with the track, even though I was only a server—then scooped Tilda into my arms. I crossed the gravel path over to the protestors' side and winced as Penny shouted at a passing couple.

"You're supporting horse murder!"

"Penny?"

She blinked at me, then lowered the megaphone as her buddies continued to chant. "Hey. You're that chick from the pub."

I nodded and edged closer.

She grinned down at Tilda. "Cute cat."

"Thanks."

Tilda hammed it up by stretching her neck out and delicately sniffing Penny's fingers before deigning to let the former jockey pet her head.

"What's up?"

I leaned closer over the barricade and lowered my voice. "I heard that you told the police you saw Jack slinking about the stables the night of the murder."

She sucked in a breath and leaned back, pale, then suddenly flushed. "How do you—I—uh—"

I raised my brows high. "Penny, I know you care about these horses. Jack's the best veterinarian here—you know how hard he works to keep them safe. If you lie and keep him detained for longer, or worse, get him convicted, you'll not only be implicating an innocent man but also putting the horses at risk."

"Ugh!" Penny let the megaphone drop to her side while she dragged her free hand down her face. She darted a glance around, then jerked her head to the side. I followed her down the barricade until we reached the dirt parking lot and stood apart from the protestors, out of earshot.

"What's this all about?"

"I'm a friend of a friend of Jack's, and I'm looking into Timmy's murder." I arched a brow. "I also care about keeping the horses safe."

Penny groaned, then shot me a pleading look. "I'm sorry! I just panicked!" She grimaced. "The truth is, I've been hooking up with an old flame who's still a jockey. We were in the stable earlier that night for a little, er..."

I raised a brow. "Roll in the hay?"

She gave me a wry grin. "Exactly." She ran a hand down her long black ponytail. "I used a fake name on the sign-in sheet so no one would know, but I guess the security guard recognized me and told the cops I was there that night."

I frowned and shifted Tilda in my arms. "So why did you tell the police you saw Jack? Did you?"

She whimpered. "No, okay?"

I raised my brows at her. "Why would you throw Jack under the bus like that? He thought you were friends."

Penny licked her lips. "I... I panicked." She edged closer, the gravel crunching under her trainers. "This animal rights group?" She jerked her head toward the shouting protestors. "They're pretty hard core. They'd freak out if they knew I was seeing anyone still on the 'inside,' as they put it. I had to give the cops something, someone, else to look into so they'd release me before word got out that I was now a suspect and the details of my personal life got out."

I shook my head. "The protestors wouldn't understand you still being, er... friends with your former colleague?"

She sniffed. "It's black and white to them. Either you're with them or against them." She shrugged. "I lost everything when I left the racing world. It was my whole life, my social circle, my career—everything!" She glanced at the animal rights group. "These people were there for me, and they're helping me spread my message about the dangers that racing poses to the horses."

She flashed her dark eyes at me. "I can't lose them, too. And if they knew about me and the guy I'm seeing, they'd think of it as a betrayal. As a former jockey, it took a lot of work to get them to accept me in the first place."

I nodded, and my heart went out to her. "That must've taken a lot of bravery to take a stand against racing, when it was all you knew." I gave her a hard look. "As much as I sympathize, you lied to the police. You've got to tell them the truth. Jack's whole life could be at stake."

She let out a heavy sigh and looked up into the bright blue sky. "I know, I know." She rolled her eyes. "I will, okay? Later."

I narrowed my eyes. "If you don't tell the police, I will."

"Ugh. Fine, now, okay? I'll go now."

"Wait!" I caught her arm as she took a few steps off. "I was curious about something; I was hoping you could help me with it?"

She crossed her arms and raised her brows. "What is it?"

I had to word my question carefully so as not to mention seeing all this in a magical vision. "I uh… noticed one jockey carrying these metal plates—" I cupped my hands to form an oval shape. "—in this kind of satchel thing, with pockets? And I was wondering what—"

"Oh, you mean the lead weights?"

I raised a brow. "Maybe?"

Penny lifted a palm. "Just about all jockeys and horses ride with them. It's a little complicated, but the gist is, for most races, every horse is supposed to carry the same amount of weight, to make it fair." She shifted on her feet. "So let's say the weight is fifty-seven kilograms."

I nodded, doing a rough translation in my head to around one hundred and twenty pounds.

"If the weight of the rider and saddle come to only fifty-five kilos, that means the rider would add another two kilograms in lead weights to the pockets of the racing saddle to reach that fifty-seven kilograms requirement."

I nodded, mulling this over. That seemed reasonable…

so why had I seen that in my vision? My heart sank a little. Maybe I just hadn't cast the spell right—I was a pretty newbie witch, after all.

Penny made a thoughtful noise. "I'm a little surprised you saw anyone using that though. The lead weights are pretty old-school. Nowadays, most jockeys use these weighted neoprene pads that go under the saddle." She shrugged. "Some guys are stuck in the old ways." She heaved a great sigh. "Well... I'm off to go talk to the police. Again."

I gave her a little wave, then Penny stalked off, handed the megaphone over to another woman, and headed for the parking lot.

I lowered Tilda to the ground and walked back to the gate beside her. I only pulled my staff pass out once I was safely past the crowd of shouting protestors. I didn't approve of Penny lying to the police, and she'd admitted to being at the stables, the scene of the crime, the night Timmy Pipe was killed. Still... I had a hard time picturing her as the killer.

She'd readily admitted to lying and seemed to be trying to do the right thing, protesting to keep horses safe. At the same time, she didn't seem as polarized as the other protestors. She was still friends with other jockeys and race staff—and was even dating one of them. I doubted she'd have killed Timmy on principle alone. Even if she wanted personal revenge for what happened to her horse and career, why now? It'd been a couple years, so why would she risk the life she'd rebuilt by going after Timmy Pipe?

I was still mulling all this over, on my way back to the tea tent, when Tilda suddenly darted left.

"Tilda!"

Follow me!

Where was my crazy cat going? I smiled apologetically as I cut across the stream of racegoers and followed her around the back of the big white tent.

I caught up with her as she was stalking around a temporary wall that blocked some dumpsters from view of the public.

"What are you doing?"

She shot me a pitying look. *Shh!*

So bossy! But she seemed like she knew what she was doing, so I obeyed her command and slowly peeked around the corner.

Cindy Watkins shook her head at Gary, her hands planted on her hips and elbows wide. "I don't care!"

Gary dabbed at his damp forehead with a kerchief and gulped. "But Halliwell is breathing down my neck!"

She huffed. "Just keep him off a little longer, yes?" She raised her brows and flashed her intense blue eyes at him. "It'll all be over tomorrow. You can handle that, right?"

It wasn't so much a question as a demand… with a threat hanging at the end of it.

Gary opened his mouth, frowned, and then pressed his lips tight together. He lowered his eyes to the ground and nodded. "Yes. Alright."

Cindy scrunched up her nose and clapped him hard on the shoulder, so that he jumped. "Good. Now, why don't you head back into the tent and have another drink on me."

I lurched back as they both turned my way and hustled toward the main thoroughfare with Tilda close at my side. My chest was heaving by the time I slipped back into the crowd, though I didn't think they'd caught me eavesdropping.

I lingered beside a table with free copies of the day's schedule to blend in, in case Cindy or Gary passed this way, and to collect my thoughts. What had they been talking about? The name Halliwell rang a bell—ah yes! Cindy's day job. Gary had said he'd been hired by her boss at Halliwell Construction.

Was Cindy wining and dining Gary on behalf of the company? Maybe—except I'd just overheard her demanding that Gary keep Halliwell off her case a little longer. What was Cindy keeping from her employer? And why would it all be over tomorrow?

Tomorrow was the last day of the races, but what did that have to do with her day job and Gary, the auditor?

I glanced down at Tilda, who sat patiently—or was it smugly— beside my feet.

"Thank you," I mouthed. Without her, I'd never have overheard those two.

You're welcome, silly billy.

It looked like a little visit to Halliwell Construction was in order.

16

HALLIWELL CONSTRUCTION

I did some sleuthing on my phone and found the number for Halliwell Construction. The racetrack crowds streamed by as the phone rang and rang, until finally a recorded message informed me that the offices were closed today.

Figured.

But the woman's message—it sounded like Cindy's voice—did suggest that if I needed to get ahold of Don Halliwell immediately, I might find him at their latest building site. I grinned as she conveniently listed the address. I hung up, summoned a ride share, and reluctantly left Tilda at the tea tent as I headed out to find Halliwell.

As I bumped along the country roads in the back seat of the little sedan, the driver's pop music blaring in the front seat, I grinned as I thought of handing Tilda over to Leo. If I had to leave her behind, at least I knew she was in good hands. Tilda had always had a soft spot for the beefy butler. Though he acted tough—puffed chest and a word of advice for everyone on how to "make gains" at the gym and eat healthier—he had a soft spot for my cat and carried her around like a baby half the time.

Rolling green hills drifted past the window, dotted with white sheep, hedgerows and the peaked rooftops of cottages and small towns in the distance. I slumped lower in the back seat, tuned out the pop music, and reviewed what I knew about the case. The races were over tomorrow, and if I had any chance of questioning all the suspects involved, I'd better do it before then.

Jack was still a possibility. He'd been furious with Timmy Pipe for disregarding his veterinary expertise and using his pull to allow Penny Zhang and her horse to race a couple of years ago. It'd ruined her career and cost that beautiful creature its life.

Jack seemed to care fiercely for his animals, but would he have killed Timmy over it? If so, why now?

Then there was Penny Zhang herself. Hopefully, she was speaking with the police now. If she hadn't followed through on her promise and told the police she'd lied, I would. Penny had access to the stable and also hated Timmy Pipe for ruining her career.

Still, in my gut, I had a hard time seeing either her or Jack being murderers.

Then there were Samar, Jemma, and her mother, Cindy. They all seemed to be in on something together—and I doubted it was just a not-so-secret engagement between the rival jockeys. In that argument between Samar and Jemma I'd overheard, Samar indicated that he and Cindy were conspiring together to protect Jemma. But from what?

Had Timmy learned about their romance and lost his cool? Or maybe he'd attacked Samar, verbally or physically, over the racing loss, and Samar had killed his trainer in a fit of rage?

I pulled my lips to the side. Quiet and polite Samar just didn't seem the type. While I didn't know much about Jemma, what I had learned seemed to suggest she didn't enjoy dirty work. I had a hard time seeing her bludgeoning a grown man to death with a shovel. Cindy seemed like she was up to something with Gary, but could she have really overpowered the famous horse trainer? And if so, why?

My head was spinning as my thoughts ran in circles—about as quickly as the horses around the track—when the car pulled to a stop. The driver didn't turn around.

"We're here."

I sat up straighter and looked out the window. We'd pulled down a small lane, bordered by fields, up to an old farmhouse and a dilapidated barn. The frame of a new one stood on a concrete foundation, with workers, tools, and a few pieces of yellow heavy machinery scattered about. This did indeed look like the building site.

I licked my lips, suddenly not so sure coming here alone had been the best idea. What if Don Halliwell was up to no good? Here I was in the middle of nowhere, about to poke my nose into his business.

I leaned forward and gripped the back of the driver seat. "Could you wait for me? I won't be long."

He half glanced back and sniffed. "You'll have to pay extra."

I nodded. "No problem. Just don't leave, okay?"

He grunted and I hoped that was a confirmation. I gulped, my throat suddenly dry, and stepped out of the car. Hammers pounded away, and a man with a nail gun framed out a doorway, his tool making a loud "thwap" sound in a steady rhythm.

About half a dozen men in boots, safety glasses, and hard hats worked away on the new barn. I squared my shoulders and crunched across the gravel driveway toward them. After several glances back, just to make sure my ride was waiting, I approached a stocky man with a clipboard who stood apart from the others, surveying the site.

I cleared my throat, and he glanced my way, his dark eyes widening with surprise.

"Hello. I'm looking for Don Halliwell?"

He cocked a brow. "Yeah. I'm him."

I'd guessed right. I stepped closer and reached out to shake his tough, calloused hand. "Minnie Wells."

He widened his stance and gave me a quick once-over. "What can I do for you, Miss Wells?"

Though his words were courteous, his clipped tone gave me the feeling that this man wouldn't spare me much of his time. I cut right to the chase.

"Does Cindy Watkins work for you?"

He waved a thick hand. "Yeah, but if you're looking for Cindy, check the horse races. She's off the clock today."

Great. I rocked on my heels, racking my brain. I probably should have spent less time reviewing suspects on the ride over and more time deciding what I'd say. I decided to try something.

"Oh!" I made a show of slapping my forehead. "You know, that's right! I was at the races today and I saw Cindy there." I gave an exaggerated roll of my eyes. "How could I forget!"

"Heh." Don Halliwell curled his lip and looked about two seconds away from turning his back on me.

"I, uh—actually saw Gary there with her. He, uh, works for you too, right?"

That got his attention. Halliwell squinted. "Gary was there?" He cocked his head. "*With* Cindy?"

I sucked on my lips and tried to ignore the deep shade of red flushing over the man's face and neck. "Mm-hmm."

His nostrils flared and he gritted his teeth. "Why, I oughtta—!" He jabbed the clipboard at the half-finished barn. "We're behind on this project, bleeding cash, and he's got the nerve to take the day off to go to the races? Bloody wanker. I'm paying his per diem to figure out why we're going under."

I raised my brows in surprise. Halliwell was going under?

He huffed and shook his head, his shoulders slumped. "Just—" He waved a palm at me. "Forget that I said that last bit, okay?"

I shot him a tight smile and nodded. "Sorry to upset you."

He waved me off. "No, thank you. Minnie Wells, right? You better believe Gary's gonna be getting an earful about this."

I nodded and backed up toward my waiting ride. "No problem. But, uh… maybe leave my name out of this?"

I wasn't sure if Halliwell had registered that. He was back to shaking his head and grumbling to himself. "—just when you think it can't get worse."

I hurried back to the car—which was thankfully still waiting for me. So Halliwell's construction firm, which Cindy managed, was going under, and he'd hired Gary to audit their books. If he wasn't aware that Cindy and Gary were spending time together—much less that Cindy was wining and dining Gary—that had to mean Cindy was up to something.

I yanked the back door to the car open and slid inside. "Thanks for waiting. I'd like to head back to the races, please."

The driver's brows raised in the rearview mirror, but without a word he cranked his radio louder and turned around in the farm's long gravel drive.

17

THE AUDIT

For what seemed like the first time since we'd arrived at the races, Carmen, the pretty chef, wasn't hanging all over Fitz. I slid past Calvin, who looked up from washing dishes to nod hello and mouth, "He's in a mood."

I fought a grin. "Fitz?"

The young butler nodded. "He's lost one of his oven mitts—you know the red ones?"

I nodded. I couldn't help being tickled by a Mr. Darcy-esque vampire being out of sorts over losing an oven mitt. "Thanks for the heads-up."

Fitz glowered as he dragged the heel of his hand through a big ball of bread dough, lifted it, and slammed it down hard.

I raised a brow as I sauntered up to him. "What'd that dough ever do to you?"

He glanced up, eyes wide, then shot me a weary smile. "Minnie."

I'd never get tired of him saying my name.

He let out a heavy sigh and threw his big flour-and-dough-covered hands in the air. "I am well aware that our tent is bringing in droves of customers, and while that will surely result in more business for the cafe back in Bath, I cannot tell you how much I loathe having to bake out of this —this—tent!"

He spat the last word like it was an insult. I had to bite my cheek to keep from smiling at his tantrum.

I took a deep breath and sidled closer. "Fitz, I know this isn't easy for you, but that's normal. We're all looking forward to getting back to Bath and our normal routine, but maybe you can think of it as an adventure?"

He softened, some of the warmth returning to his dark eyes, and returned to kneading the dough. "Hmph. Well, to me, a nice warm cup of tea and a good book is plenty of adventure."

I grinned. "Can't disagree with you there." Then again, this was coming from two people who'd crossed the notorious vampire council and chased down more than one murderer. We probably both had more than our fair share of adventure on a regular basis.

I leaned against the flour-dusted counter beside him and crossed my arms. "So. I paid Don Halliwell a visit at a construction site. He's Cindy's boss at her day job."

Fitz looked up, his brows pinched together. "When?"

I shrugged. "Just now."

His lips parted. "But you didn't tell me you were leaving."

"Yeah... it was kind of impromptu."

He blinked, his eyes full of concern. "Who'd you take with you?"

I hunched up my shoulders and winced. He wasn't going to like this. "The rideshare driver?"

Fitz's nostrils flared and he leaned closer, smelling of bread and cinnamon. *Yum.*

"I fear you have put yourself in danger, Minnie."

I nodded. "You're right. I'll bring someone along next time." I grinned at him. "You'd be my first choice, but you were busy."

His throat bobbed and his cheeks blushed. He shook himself. "I mean more than just your visit to the construction site. Horse racing involves fortunes and powerful people." He frowned as his eyes searched my face. "And you seem to be positioning yourself in the middle of some nefarious dealings."

I grinned, trying not to giggle at Fitz's old-fashioned vocabulary. "Hey, I've got power too." I wiggled my fingers, indicating my magic.

He flashed his dark eyes as he fought a smile. "You do, indeed, but a man was killed." All the humor left his expression as he caught my eye. "Promise me you'll be careful."

I nodded, words escaping me as I stared into the dark pools of his eyes. My gaze dropped to his full lips, and I gulped, shaking myself back to the present. "I will. I know." I nodded and blew out a breath, trying to keep my mind off thoughts of kissing my vampire boss.

Fitz straightened and resumed working the dough, dragging the heel of his hand through, flipping it, and dragging again. Why was that so sexy?

"Well, Don Halliwell seemed to have no idea that Gary and Cindy knew each other. And he got pretty miffed when I mentioned seeing Gary at the races. He said something about the business going under and him paying Gary to audit the books?"

Fitz nodded. "It's likely Halliwell's experiencing financial issues and has hired Gary to check all of their accounts."

Fitz shook his head, a single wavy lock tumbling over his forehead. He tried to blow it back, since his hands were covered in flour, but it didn't cooperate. It took effort to resist the urge to reach up and brush it back for him.

I was at work. *Be professional, Minnie.*

Fitz clarified. "It's possible someone is stealing from the business accounts... or at the very least, mismanaging them."

My eyes widened. "Cindy! She's Halliwell's office manager, which means she's probably in charge of keeping the books."

Fitz raised his thick brows. "Her boss would likely disapprove of her schmoozing the auditor then."

I smirked. Something about Fitz saying "schmoozing" tickled me.

"I suspect she's got something to hide."

"So Cindy's bribing Gary with VIP treatment and bottomless mimosas so he won't uncover the fact that she's been stealing money from her day job?"

I narrowed my eyes and replayed that argument I'd overheard between Jemma and Samar. "Samar mentioned something about a money scheme that was going to get Jemma in trouble." I bit my lip and gazed up at Fitz's chiseled face. "You think he could've been talking about Cindy stealing from Halliwell?"

Fitz nodded, his gaze thoughtful. "Could be."

I nibbled my thumb tip. "But why would Cindy steal from the construction firm? She's a successful, famous horse breeder—does she really need the money that badly?" I frowned. "And that argument I overheard—Jemma claimed she didn't know what Samar was talking about, but what if she was lying? Could Jemma be the one behind the theft? She does have a reputation for enjoying the finer things in life—maybe she had to steal from her mom's employer to support that lifestyle?"

Fitz nodded. "That's possible. In any case, it seems likely that Cindy Watkins is showering Gary with her generous hospitality in an attempt to keep him from discovering her, or her daughter's, embezzlement."

"Or from reporting it." I sucked in a breath. "I overheard Cindy ordering Gary to hold Halliwell off for one more day." I frowned. "That seems to imply that Gary's aware of the theft. But if she's been cooking the books, what's one more day going to do for her?"

Fitz shot me a serious look. "Tomorrow's the last day of the races—the finals for the Cheltenham Cup."

I opened my mouth to ask him what that might mean in relation to the embezzlement and the murder, when Carmen waltzed back in. She wore a low tank top that made even me stare and shot Fitz a dazzling smile before slipping back into her white chef's jacket.

"Thanks for holding down the fort while I took my lunch break." She winked at my boss before shooting me a flat look.

Guess that was my cue.

I had enough going on with trying to solve this case and free Jack from jail. I didn't need the extra stress of having to witness her shameless flirting. I patted the counter.

"I'm going to bring Mim a cup of coffee."

Fitz's gaze lingered on my face. "That's kind of you."

I grinned and raised my brows. "We both know she could use a little pick-me-up."

He nodded. "Be careful, Minnie."

"Always." I grabbed a mug from the dish rack and filled it up with steaming, dark brown coffee—Mim liked it black—before heading out into the stands to track down my mentor.

I knew she had to be exhausted from charming the horses to keep them safe—hopefully the coffee would help a bit. Plus, I wanted to fill her in on my visit to Don Halliwell.

I PERCHED on the hard seat beside Mim as she guzzled the coffee I'd brought her. The announcer's voice blared over the loudspeakers as he introduced the next race and lineup of horses and jockeys. Mim lowered the cup from her lips and let out a heavy sigh.

"Bless you." She patted my knee, and I grinned. She shot me an arch look. "Maybe next time a little something stronger in the mug, though?" She winked.

"Not sure we have anything in the kitchen besides champagne, but I'll see if I can find something for you." I narrowed my eyes with concern at her bloodshot gaze and pale skin. "For real—are you doing okay?"

My mentor was an experienced and capable witch, but I feared she might be pushing herself too hard.

"I know you want to protect the horses, but you've got to look after yourself too."

She squeezed my hand with her own ring-covered one and gave me a weak smile. "I'll be fine, poppet. I'll need a spa week after this, but I'll make it through." She shook her head as she drew her crocheted shawl tighter around her shoulders. "I'd never forgive myself if I took a break and something happened to one of these lovely creatures."

I followed her gaze to the track below, where the horses and jockeys gathered behind the starting line. A few horses snorted and shook their heads, their coats shiny and rippling with muscle. My shoulders slumped—I'd probably feel the same way, but I was worried about my friend and mentor.

"Now, stop fretting and tell me what you've discovered before the race starts."

I nodded as Mim continued to sip from her mug. "First of all, you were right. Penny admitted to lying about seeing Jack in the stables."

She spluttered on her coffee, then shook a finger at no one in particular. "I knew it!"

"I convinced her to go tell the police the truth."

The older witch sighed. "I hope it helps. But there's still the issue of Jack's fingerprints on the shovel. I'm afraid it might not be enough to get him released."

I filled Mim in on my visit to the construction site. "Me and Fitz talked it over, and we think Cindy's hiding something at her day job. Fitz suggested she might be embezzling money, which would explain why her boss, Don Halliwell, hired Gary to audit the books."

Mim's faint brows rose high up her forehead. "That explains why she's bribing him with mimosas and the star treatment—to keep him from exposing her."

I scooted closer. "And I told you I overheard Samar and Jemma arguing yesterday. I got the sense that Samar thought he was saving Jemma from getting in big trouble. Maybe she's in on the embezzlement?" I shrugged. "I also overheard Cindy ordering Gary to hold Halliwell off for one more day, but I don't get why one day would make a difference."

Mim spluttered into her coffee. She lowered the mug and shot me a wide-eyed look. "If Jemma and Cindy win the Cup, they get the one-hundred-thousand-pound prize money."

I gasped. "So she could pay back what she's stolen from Halliwell before he notices it's gone?"

Mim nodded. "Not to mention the prestige and earnings she'll make off breeding a winning horse."

I sank back in the hard seat and marveled. "So if Cindy and Jemma win tomorrow, it'll solve all their money problems." I sighed. "I still don't see a connection to Timmy Pipe's murder, though."

Mim nodded slowly, her gaze far away as she mulled it over.

I counted our top suspects off on my fingers. "Penny claims she has an alibi—"

"And Jack didn't do it."

I nodded. "Which leaves us with Samar, Cindy, and Jemma, who all claimed they were together that night, celebrating the young couple's engagement."

Mim shook her head, which sent her corkscrew curls bouncing over her shoulders. "You've got to figure out if they're telling the truth."

I nodded and edged a little closer, keeping my voice low, though I doubted any of the spectators around us could eavesdrop over the roar of the crowd and the blaring speakers. "I also tried scrying."

"Oh! Well done, doll! And?"

I pouted. "I saw something about lead racing weights being put into a saddle."

"Could you see whose saddle?"

I shook my head. "Does that mean anything to you?"

The older witch frowned. "No. Sorry, dear."

I sucked in a breath. I should probably just chalk it up to bad spell casting. After all, I'd asked to see what happened to Timmy Pipe and instead had gotten a peek at the jockeys' locker room. Something had clearly gone awry.

Mim patted my leg. "Alright, dear, races are about to start up again. I've got to concentrate."

I gave her a tight smile and rose, then shuffled my way back down the row of spectators towards the tearoom tent. I felt like all the pieces were there—I just couldn't see how they fit together.

18

UP IN FLAMES

I spent the rest of the day helping Fitz and the butlers work the tent and keeping an eye on Gary. He stayed at his table most of the day, indulging in all the delicious scones and various treats Fitz specialized in. Plus, plenty of mimosas.

Penny Zhang popped in to tell me she'd spoken with the police, but that they'd seemed determined to still pin the crime on Jack. It seemed Mim's fears were warranted.

I'd hoped to have a chance to get more information about Cindy or Jemma, but before I knew it, we were cleaning up for the night and heading back to the inn. My sleuthing would have to wait until tomorrow.

After a delicious dinner, sandwiched in a booth between Fitz and Leo, we all said our goodnights and headed upstairs to our rooms. I barely mustered the energy to brush my teeth and wash my face before I collapsed into bed with a purring Tilda at my side.

I GROANED and rolled onto my side.

Wake up, silly snake! Wake up!

I squeezed my eyes shut tighter and whimpered as I pulled my pillow over my head. Was it time to get up already? It felt as though I'd just closed my eyes.

Tilda smacked at the pillow—and my head underneath it.

Get up now! Don't you smell it?

I huffed out a sigh, weary to my bones. As much as I loved this new ability to hear my familiar, was there an off button? Or at least a way to turn the volume down in my head?

But then her words sank in. Smell what? I sniffed. Was that... smoke?

Tilda frantically batted at my head as I opened my eyes wide and shot bolt upright in bed.

She leapt back. *Finally!*

"Oh no, oh no!" I threw the covers back and stumbled to my feet, fumbling for the lamp on the bedside table and knocking my phone to the ground before I managed to turn the light on. Tilda paced back and forth at the foot of the bed, her hackles raised and tail slicing the air.

I scooped her into my arms, and barefoot, in my sleep tee and shorts, bolted for the door. I hesitated as I got closer, the heat radiating through the door almost unbearable even from a few feet away.

My chest heaved. Fire. The heat must mean it was right outside my door.

The window, silly.

I ducked my chin to give Tilda a hasty kiss on her head, then hurried to the old casement window. I flipped the latch to unlock it, then cranked it open, with my familiar tucked under my other arm. Once it was cracked wide enough to slip through, I hesitated and turned back.

What about Fitz and my friends? They were all staying here with me. Should I call them? Bang on the walls?

RIIINNNNGGGG!

A deafeningly loud fire alarm sounded, and though I winced, I was grateful. No way could anyone sleep through that—not even Al, who bragged he could fall asleep at the drop of a hat and slept like a baby. I said a silent wish that everyone would get out safely, then saw to rescuing myself and Tilda first.

I leaned out the window, and my stomach churned. The inn was a charmingly old historic building—which meant no fire escapes. I gazed down at a sharply peaked roof covered in flat shingles that looked horribly slippery. I turned my head right and left, hoping for some tree to shimmy down, but no such luck. We were three stories up, with nothing but a steep roof—and a long fall—below us.

I glanced back at the door to the hall, then looked out into the night again. Sirens sounded in the distance. Good. There'd be a fire truck here soon—but would it be soon enough?

I'll be okay.

I nodded and eased Tilda out the window, setting her gingerly on the shingles. Agile as always, she turned her bright yellow eyes to me.

Hurry. Don't be a scaredy cat.

I raised a brow as I grasped the windowsill and hiked my knee up. "Easy for you to say. You're used to walking on roofs." That's how she'd come to me at Gus's place, all those months ago. I frowned and looked around—where'd she run off to? Oh well, I hoped she'd gotten herself to safety.

The moon shone full and bright for me to see by, which

was one positive in this terrible situation. Willing myself to breathe and keep moving, I eased one leg out onto the chilly, moss-covered roof, then spun to face the window. I grasped the sill tightly as I dragged my other leg out, then looked around.

Great. I was kneeling on a slick, steep roof three stories up with no way down.

Tilda trotted down from the peak and nuzzled against my side. *It's okay, silly witch. We'll get you down safely. Just follow me. There's a tree on the other side we can climb down.*

"I'd give you a hug, but I'm too afraid to let go." My fingers ached from clutching the sill.

Tail swishing with agitation Tilda led the way up the steep peak. *Hurry, though. The flames are spreading.*

Perfect.

Sweating despite the chill in the night air, I crawled up the slippery, moss-covered roof on my hands and knees. My heart thundered in my chest, and waves of fear and dizziness washed over me so that I had to stop, squeeze my eyes shut, and then will myself to go on. I was near the top, where Tilda waited for me, silhouetted against the moon, when a shingle came loose under my knee.

I screamed and slid several feet down but clawed my way to a stop. My arms and legs trembled as I lay spread eagle, stretched out across the roof to keep from falling.

It's okay. Try again.

I squeezed my eyes shut and shook my head. "Go on, Tilda. Get yourself safe. I'll—I'll be right behind you."

I fought to get my breathing back under control. And my body. My limbs absolutely refused to cooperate as I clung to the mossy shingles.

A rough tongue scraped across my cheek, and I peeled an eye open. Tilda stood nose to nose with me, her yellow eyes glowing in the moonlight. *You're a witch, remember? Use magic.*

Tears streamed down my cheeks. I'd made so much progress with Mim, but we'd never covered anything that would help me in a situation like this. Had we? I tried to think of *anything* that'd be useful, but fear seemed to have wiped my mind blank. I needed help.

A loud thud sounded from somewhere below me, followed by shattering glass.

"Minnie?"

"Fitz!" I'd never been more grateful to hear his voice.

Tilda perked her ears and gazed behind me with wide eyes. I started to turn my head to look, but a wave of dizziness overtook me as I glimpsed how high up I was. Instead, I snapped my eyes shut and pressed my cheek against the cold, wet roof.

Several quick thuds, and suddenly a pair of shiny leather brogues stood in front of my face. I risked a glance up to find Fitz standing over me, as if it was the easiest thing in the world. He crouched down and looked me over with concern, his dark brows pinched together and eyes worried. A single wavy lock fell across his forehead, though the rest of his hair was more mussed than usual.

"Are you hurt?"

I shook my head. "No. Just scared of heights."

He gave a terse nod. "Don't be afraid. I'm here." He swiftly and gently slid his arms around me and drew me towards him. Tilda leapt onto my stomach, and then Fitz stood, cradling me. I slung one arm around his chilly neck and hugged Tilda close with my other.

In a flash, we were off. He sprinted up and over the peak of the roof, then leapt to a branch of a big oak tree and from there to the soft, grassy ground. It happened so fast that I didn't breathe until we'd landed safely. I suddenly had the urge to drop to my knees and kiss the ground, like they did in the movies. I gazed up at Fitz, his chiseled face illuminated by the moon and golden flames.

Maybe it wasn't the *ground* I wanted to kiss....

The romantic moment was interrupted as Tilda leapt off me, gracefully landing on the soft grass. Fitz hugged me to him and dashed (at a more human pace) around to the front of the inn, where a crowd gathered and watched the flames engulf the top story of the inn. Glass shattered as orange flames licked at the sill. Was that my window that just exploded?

"Fitz! Minnie!"

To my utter relief, the guys waved us over. Leo, Al, Calvin, Dominic, and Cho huddled together in their boxers and pajamas, hair mussed and faces creased with sleep lines from their pillows. We joined them, everyone too shocked and dazed to speak much. Fitz placed me softly on my feet, and I shot him a grateful look.

"Is everyone out?"

He narrowed his eyes and peered up at the old building, no doubt searching for people who might be trapped inside with his superhuman senses. I'd never been so struck by how much like superheroes vampires could be. I fought a grin, despite the dire circumstances, as I took in his outfit. He'd probably never gone to sleep—Fitz seemed to function just fine on almost none at all—and still wore his full butler uniform, coattails and all. While the rest of the guests looked weary and disheveled, my boss looked ready to attend a ball.

Finally, he nodded.

"I believe everyone's safe, yes."

My shoulders sagged with relief. While this was still

terrifying and a great loss, it could have been a lot more tragic. The sirens grew louder, and multiple fire trucks rushed to the scene. We were ushered back from the inn and watched as dawn lightened the sky, until they put out the flames.

My head ached, and I cradled Tilda in my arms—my little familiar had saved my life, with Fitz's help—when the firefighters were joined by other uniformed officers—the police. As they conferred, Fitz's brows raised.

I leaned close. "What'd you hear?"

His throat bobbed. "They're positive it was arson." Fitz's lips pressed into a grim line. "Remind me, which room number were you staying in?"

I frowned, willing my sleep-deprived brain to work. My adrenaline dump had evaporated, leaving me woozy with sleepiness. "Um... three-oh-two."

Fitz's dark eyes held mine. "They believe the fire was started right outside your door."

19

CONTINENTAL BREAKFAST

The next morning, exhausted and still coughing from all the smoke inhalation, Fitz, the guys and I gathered over a continental breakfast. While the chain hotel we'd been moved to didn't have the same old-world charm as the inn, I was grateful that we'd found somewhere to stay for the night. Especially considering how booked up everywhere was with the races.

My stomach tightened as I pushed cereal around my chipped bowl with a spoon. Considering that today was the last day of the races—and we'd almost gone down in flames last night—the pressure to catch Timmy Pipe's killer weighed heavily on me and twisted my stomach. I set my spoon down, finally accepting that I had no appetite, and looked up to find Fitz studying my face.

I shot him a weak smile, then turned to address the other guys. Leo looked disdainfully down at his bowl of fruit and bacon, then back at the breakfast bar. "They have practically nothing but carbs."

Al, who was happily scarfing his third muffin, smirked. "Watching your girlish figure?"

Cho snickered, and even Dominic cracked a smile.

Calvin laid his freckled cheek in his hand, his eyelids flickering as he fought to stay awake.

I cleared my throat, and they looked my way. I leaned forward over the two rectangular tables that we'd pushed together and lowered my voice so the other diners and wait-staff wouldn't overhear.

"I think Timmy Pipe's killer came after me last night."

A muscle twitched in Dom's cheek. "The firefighters said the fire was started right outside your door, right?"

I nodded, and Fitz confirmed it. "I overheard them say as much."

Dom shook his head. "Why you?"

I sucked in a breath and stroked Tilda, who lay curled up in my lap. For the thousandth time I sent her a mental "thank you" for waking me up in time to escape. "I think they knew I was on their trail and wanted to keep me quiet."

Leo and I locked eyes, and he lowered a piece of bacon from his mouth. "Do you know who it is?"

I let out something between a chuckle and a whimper. "That's the worst part—no!"

Fitz kept his eyes glued to my face. "But you did figure something out, didn't you?"

I raised my brows and stroked Tilda's soft fur. "You mean about the embezzling?" I filled in the guys on what I'd learned the day before. "So we think Cindy's been stealing money from her day job, and she's bribing Gary to keep from reporting her to her boss, Halliwell." I shrugged. "We think she's banking on Jemma winning the cup, and the prize money to go with it, in order to pay Halliwell back. But I can't figure out how it's connected to Timmy Pipe's murder... or why Cindy's been stealing in the first place."

Dom laced his huge hands together and leaned forward.

"Horses are expensive." He splayed his palms. "Breeders must have some massive startup costs."

"Huh." I leaned forward, too. "So maybe Cindy was stealing from Halliwell to fund her stables?"

Dom nodded slowly. "That's my best guess."

Fitz and I exchanged approving looks. "I think it's a good one."

Al spoke around the muffin in his mouth. "What's that got to do with the murder, though?"

Cho pointed at him. "That's the million-pound question."

Calvin sniffed and jerked upright. "What'd I miss?"

I giggled. He'd clearly been asleep. Still, looking around the table, I felt so grateful that not only had we all survived what I suspected was an attempt on my life, but that these guys were truly my friends and trying to help me solve the case. I'd come a long way since feeling so lonely and unlucky after my divorce. Now I had great friends that felt like a little family.

Fitz shifted in his seat. "So Cindy, and possibly Jemma, are betting on winning the cup today in order to avoid having their embezzlement detected."

Leo reached for Tilda, who happily leapt into his arms. "Seems risky."

Dom scoffed. "Not really. With Samar and Jane Austen out of the final race, Jemma Watkins and Little Grey Goose are all but shoo-ins to win."

I froze as something clicked in my mind. I whirled to face Fitz, whose eyes had widened, likely coming to the same realization I had. A slow grin spread across his lips. "They're all but guaranteed to win."

I smiled, my heart pounding with excitement. "Because Samar and Jane Austen, their only real competition, are out of the race."

"You want to clue the rest of us in?" Cho held his spoon in the air.

Fitz and I spun to face the others, who all leaned in around the table.

I caught Dom's eye. "Jane Austen ran badly that first day of the races, right?"

He frowned. "Yeah. It was surprising. I've watched replays and listened to commentators' takes. No one can figure out what happened. It's not like she stumbled or Samar rode badly, but Jane Austen just couldn't seem to keep up."

I grinned and nodded. "Okay, I don't know how he did it exactly, but what if Samar threw the race?"

"You mean—" Calvin stifled a yawn. "—he lost on purpose?"

Leo scoffed. "Why would he do that?"

There was a beat of silence, and then we all spoke at once.

"Jemma!"

An older couple at a table nearby looked our way, and I shot them an apologetic grin, while Al raised his hand in a wave.

"So because they're in love and he wants to help her?"

I grinned at Calvin. Of course the sweet kid would come up with the most altruistic answer.

"Psh!" Cho scoffed. "Or because she's using him."

Both seemed like possibilities. By Penny's account, Jemma was stuck-up and used to living a rich lifestyle. I could see a selfish person like that using a sweet guy like Samar to keep her and her mother out of prison. Then again, during that argument I overheard between Samar and Jemma, she'd sounded sincere when she told him she loved him. Plus, she hadn't seemed to know what Samar was talking about in regards to her mother.

I shrugged. "Maybe Jemma isn't even aware of the trouble her mother's in. Maybe Cindy's the one manipulating Samar and holding her daughter over his head to get him to lose, so they can win."

Dom drummed his fingers on the Formica table. "Like I said, I've rewatched that race several times... and the coverage afterwards. Timmy Pipe was furious with Samar for the loss." He raised a brow significantly and glanced around at all of us. "What if Timmy Pipe figured out that Samar lost on purpose?"

"Oof." Al winced. "Not good."

I tapped a finger to my lips. I could imagine Timmy confronting Samar, verbally attacking him... maybe physically attacking him too.

I covered my mouth. "That would explain Samar's black eye. Maybe his trainer punched him."

"Yeah." Leo nodded as he snuggled with Tilda, who now lay purring in his lap. "Timmy attacks Samar. Samar fights back, and he accidentally kills Timmy Pipe."

Fitz sat up straighter, still decked out in his butler gear that reeked of smoke. His was the only uniform that had survived the fire. All the rest of us were in street clothes donated by the firefighters. I hoped to get out of my oversized sweatpants and Looney Tunes T-shirt soon, by making a run to the local shops for an outfit.

My vampire boss leaned forward, his elbows on the table. "Perhaps Samar sought out Jemma and Cindy and they assisted him in covering up his crime." He tipped his head. "It'd be in Cindy's best interest to keep it quiet, given that the fight between Samar and Timmy was started because Samar purposefully lost the race on her behalf."

"And that would lead the police right back to her and the money she stole from Halliwell." I scoffed. "Guys. I think we're onto something here."

Al pointed his croissant at me. "Yes, but the proof is in the pudding." He grew dreamy. "Pudding sounds good..."

I grinned at him as Calvin nodded. "Al's right. Do we have any proof?"

I shook my head. "Samar signed into the stable security sheet around that time, but so did Jack, Cindy, Jemma, and probably half a dozen other staff."

"And no witnesses?"

I shook my head at Leo.

We all ate in silence (except for Fitz, who only pretended to eat) for several moments, all lost in thought. We didn't have any proof. We could probably get Gary to spill about the embezzlement, but that didn't directly tie Cindy—or anyone, for that matter—to Timmy's murder. And with today being the last day of the races, my time for finding proof was running out. Plus, I'd almost been killed last night. If I was going to keep snooping around to catch the murderer, I'd better do it fast, before they had another chance to strike.

Cho smirked. "It'd just be so much easier if Samar would confess, right?"

Al played along. "Is that so much to ask?"

"Wait!" I pointed at Cho. "That's it."

He shot me a pitying look. "I was kidding, Minnie. That's not going to happen."

I grinned at Fitz, who gave me an encouraging nod. "Okay, but what if it is? What if there's a way to get Samar to confess?"

Leo tipped his head. "Why would he do that?"

I sat up straighter, feeling rather proud of myself in my

Tweety Bird tee. “For the same reason he lost the race in the first place.”

“Ooh!” Cho rubbed his palms together. “She’s got a plan!”

20

CONFESSIONS

Within a couple of hours of breakfast—and after grabbing a new outfit each at the local shop—the plan was in place. We'd called the police, as well as track officials, and arranged to meet up in the stables, outside the stall where Timmy Pipe had been murdered. Yellow police tape still cordoned off the area, but glancing inside made me shudder. I could still picture the trainer's lifeless body among the hay.

While Fitz and the other butlers still had to work the tent, I'd borrowed Leo and Cho to come with me and Mim, who I'd convinced to leave off charming the horses for a few minutes. I couldn't help but pace, nervous, as we waited for the others to show up.

Cho waggled his brows at me. "This is pretty exciting."

I whimpered. "That's one word for it. Nerve-wracking is another."

Leo shot me a reassuring look as he cradled Tilda in his arms. "You've got this. You've done it before."

Mim squeezed my shoulder. "I know you'll get Jack free."

I sure hoped so. I felt the pressure of clearing his name,

and my whole theory was riding on a good guess and a bet that love would make the truth come out.

Shadowy figures darkened the end of the aisle, and Detectives Bennett and Calle stepped closer, flanked by several uniformed officers and Jack. Mim rushed into his arms, and they embraced.

I was grateful to see he was no longer cuffed, and though he had bags under his eyes, he still winked at me. I grinned back. Good—he had some of his fire back.

Detective Bennett shot me an arch look. "You were right about the first part."

I gaped. "You found evidence of the embezzling?"

She tipped her head at her quiet partner, who held up a small stack of notebooks in her gloved hands.

I grinned at Cho and Leo. We were halfway there... now for the tough part.

Detective Bennett gave me a hard look. "Let's hope you were right about the rest."

Moments later, Cindy, Jemma, and Samar strode toward us, accompanied by a couple of track officials in identical navy suit jackets emblazoned with the Derbyshire Downs logo.

An older official with a thick mustache furrowed his bushy brows as his eyes landed on the officers. "What's this about now?"

Jemma cocked her hip and tossed her long blond ponytail, which was tied, as usual, with a blue ribbon. "I have to race in less than an hour—this is absurd!" Though she jutted her chin in the air, her eyes widened with fear.

Cindy crossed her arms and shot daggers at me, while Samar paled and looked like he might be ill.

The famous horse breeder's voice dripped with contempt. "There had better be a good reason for this."

I gulped. We were still missing a couple of important people. I glanced back at Detective Bennett. "Is he coming or…?"

I was interrupted by a stocky middle-aged man charging up from behind the officers. "Hallo? I came as quick as I could get away from the building site."

I fought a grin and glanced at Cindy in time to catch the fear that flickered across her face. She quickly regrouped and shot her boss, Don Halliwell, a pleasant smile. "Don? I didn't realize you'd be attending the races today."

The tanned builder sidled up beside the uniformed officers and folded his thick arms. "Can someone please tell me what this is about?"

Cindy lifted her nose in the air. "Yes. Please."

My stomach tightened with nerves as our final player in this drama arrived—Gary, the auditor, escorted by an officer. Judging by the white linen napkin still tucked into his collar, they'd just pulled him away from the tea tent.

Halliwell startled. "Gary! What are you doing here? Did I not make myself clear yesterday, when I told you and Cindy that you were to be at your hotel or our offices, looking over the books?"

Gary's face flushed bright red. He pressed his lips tight together and avoided Halliwell's eyes by staring down at his shoes.

His sheepish reaction only gave me more confidence that my theory was correct. I blew out a shaky breath—I sure hoped so. I glanced at Detective Bennet, who raised her dark brows and swept a hand in my direction. I took that as permission to get started with my accusations. I'd explained enough to get her and the other officers and suspects here—now I had to prove it was worth it.

I cleared my throat and stepped forward. All eyes locked

on me, and I fought against my nerves. Suddenly, a wave of calm rushed over me—my shoulders relaxed, and I took a full, easy breath.

Meow.

I glanced down as Tilda trotted up and nuzzled my ankles. I shot her a grateful look. With her help, I could do this. I lifted my gaze and found Cindy's.

"The police have found your cooked books."

Don Halliwell sputtered, "C-Cooked books?" He gawked at Cindy and threw a hand at me. "What's she talking about?"

The track officials looked at Cindy with interest as well.

The blond forced a tight smile. "I have no idea what this *waitress* is talking about." She scoffed at the detectives. "This is nonsense! We have a race to win. Come, Jemma."

She turned on her heel, but Detective Bennet narrowed her eyes. "Stop right there. You will stay here until we dismiss you." She nodded at me to continue.

I looked at the horse breeder, trying to project more confidence than I felt. "You can't lie your way through this one, Cindy. You've been embezzling money from your day job at Halliwell Construction."

Detective Calle held up the stack of notebooks. "Hundreds of thousands of dollars, in fact. We obtained a rush warrant to search your stables and found two sets of books for Halliwell Construction in your files."

"The falsified books you showed your employer and the real ones—which showed exactly how much money you've stolen over the years." Detective Bennett leveled Cindy a hard look. "Turns out you've been using the stolen money to fund your stables, correct?"

Jemma whirled to face Cindy, her eyes and mouth wide. "Mother!"

While Cindy gritted her jaw and glared at the detectives, Don Halliwell lurched forward, fuming. "You've been my employee for fifteen years. I trusted you!" His broad chest heaved as he gaped at the stable owner. "You said we were taking a hit the last several years because of high union wages and equipment costs, but you were stealing it?"

Cindy waved her hands and tried for a pleasant smile. "Don. It's not how it seems. I can explain, you see—"

But Don, red-faced and trembling, pointed at Gary, who looked like he wanted to disappear. "You were supposed to audit our books." He gestured between the two of them. "What is this?"

I jumped in to explain my theory. "Cindy was wining and dining Gary to bribe him into overlooking her embezzlement."

Cindy's lips curled back from her teeth, and I edged back a bit. Despite the presence of the police, I wasn't entirely sure she wouldn't try to attack me.

I turned to her. "I overheard you asking Gary to give you until the end of today. You just needed to win the Derbyshire Cup, and then you could use the purse money to repay what you stole from Halliwell."

Cindy rolled her eyes. "*Borrowed*, is more like it."

Gary whimpered and clasped his hands together at his chest, as though imploring everyone to take pity on him. "I'm sorry! My life is just so boring! I always play by the books, but how has that worked out for me? I'm divorced, and my kids don't talk to me!"

Cindy bared her teeth and hissed, "Shut up, you stupid man!"

Gary's shoulders slumped, and he jutted his bottom lip out. "I got to be a VIP at the biggest races in the country for a few days!" He thumbed at Cindy. "And she tipped me off about the race. I've got a huge bet riding on the cup race since I knew Jemma would win."

Don Halliwell's color faded, and he looked like he'd aged about twenty years, his anger replaced by disappointment and betrayal. He shook his head, his voice quiet. "You're both unbelievable."

Detective Bennet cleared her throat. "Looks like we have plenty of evidence to make arrests on the embezzlement charges." She stepped her feet wider and shot me a challenging look. "But what does this have to do with Timmy Pipe's murder?"

I glanced at Cho and Leo, who gave me encouraging nods, and Tilda purred at my feet. Emboldened by my friends, I continued on with the part of my theory I wasn't entirely sure about. "Cindy needed to win the cup race and the prize money. While her daughter is good, she needed a *guarantee*. At some point, Cindy discovered her daughter Jemma's secret engagement to Samar and used that to her advantage."

Samar turned to Cindy, his big dark eyes welling with tears. "You told me Jemma was wrapped up in the embezzlement scheme." He set his jaw, his face pinched with hurt. "But it was all *you*?"

Jemma covered her mouth and shook her head at her mom.

Cindy sniffed and looked toward the dusty rafters. "Jemma spends *my* money. *I* house and feed her and provide for her training and career. Of course it concerned her."

Samar pointed a shaking finger at Cindy. "You told me Jemma would go to jail unless she won the race and could pay back Halliwell with the prize money!" Tears streamed down his face. "You lied!"

Jemma looked between her aloof mother and panicking fiancé. "Mum! How could you?" She turned back to Samar. "I had no idea about any of this till just now."

Samar hung his head. "I'm a fool. I'd do anything for you —and your mother knew it and used it against me."

I jumped in to fill in the gaps—hoping I was right. "So you lost the race on purpose."

Samar nodded, his face full of anguish.

Cindy sneered. "Prove it."

"Oh boy." One of the track officials shifted on his feet, an uncomfortable grimace on his face.

I pressed on, hoping I could get a confession out of Samar or Jemma. "Timmy Pipe figured it out."

Samar, his eyes on the ground, nodded—confirming my guess.

I pressed my lips together. "And that knowledge is what ultimately got him killed."

Samar and Jemma locked eyes, and then Samar stepped toward me and the detectives. "I confess!" His throat bobbed. "I killed Timmy. It was me."

I stared at him, somewhat softened. He really did love Jemma. Because I had a strong suspicion that he was taking the fall to protect her once again. Just like he'd agreed to Cindy's race fixing scheme when he thought it would keep his fiancé out of trouble.

Jemma burst forward and wrapped Samar in a tight hug before lifting her little nose in the air and addressing the detectives. "I can't let him do this. It was me. I killed that horrible man, Timmy Pipe."

Samar shook his head at her. "Jemma, don't."

Tears streaked down her cheeks. "I love you. You can't sacrifice for me anymore."

If I'd been surprised by Samar's sacrifice, I was shocked

by Jemma's. I exchanged wide-eyed looks with Leo and Cho. While I'd heard rumors about Jemma being stuck-up and entitled, whatever else she might be, she was truly in love with Samar.

The stoic Detective Bennett seemed less impressed with the display. She folded her arms and shot the young couple a withering look. "Explain."

Jemma angled herself between the cops and Samar. "Timmy figured out that Samar lost on purpose."

Detective Bennett narrowed her eyes. "How?"

Jemma and Samar exchanged looks and then Samar dropped his gaze. "I added extra weights to my saddle to slow Jane Austen down. I paid off one of the officials to let it slide when we weighed in."

I covered my mouth to stifle a gasp. My vision! I'd done the spell correctly after all. I'd seen Samar adding the lead weights so he'd lose the race without it being obvious to commentators and analysts that he'd done anything to throw it.

Samar toed the ground with his black riding boots. "I tried to sneak the weights off afterwards, but Timmy was on my case, and I didn't get a chance." His chin trembled, and Jemma rubbed his back. "He—he must've found them, because he cornered me in the stall that night. He had one of the weights in his hand and—" Tears streamed down the young jockey's face, and he gulped. "And he started screaming at me. He told me he'd figured out my little plan to lose so that Jemma could win."

Samar's chest heaved. "He didn't know about Cindy's part in it. He just thought I was fixing to lose because Jemma was manipulating me. I've never seen him so enraged. He told me he was going to kill me." Samar lifted his palms, as if pleading with us to understand. "I believed him. I tried to cry out, but I was terrified. He—he used the weight to hit me." His hand trembled as he touched his bruised cheek.

I sucked on my lips, full of pity for him. Samar had really been placed between a rock and a hard place.

He sniffled and glanced at his fiancée. "Jemma saved me. I really think Timmy would've killed me if she hadn't intervened."

The two jockeys exchanged looks, and then Jemma, ashen, took a breath and lifted her chin. "I walked up about the time Timmy started threatening to kill him. I saw him hit Samar with the lead weight, and I just reacted. There was a shovel nearby, so I picked it up and hit him over the head."

She sniffled. "I didn't mean to kill him. I just wanted to stop him from hurting Samar."

Detectives Bennett and Calle exchanged looks, as if a whole silent conversation was happening between them. This had to change things. If Jemma had acted in defense of Samar, that had to count for something. It wasn't like she'd murdered Timmy in cold blood—by all accounts, Samar would've wound up dead by his trainer's hand if she hadn't acted.

Still... something about their stories nagged at my mind.

Jemma buried her face in her hands, and her shoulders shook with sobs. Samar rubbed her back, but Cindy tutted and strode forward, pulling her daughter into her arms and stroking her blond hair. "There, there. My poor girl."

Samar looked like he'd like to cut in but hung back.

Bennet's voice was flat. "What then?"

Samar sniffled. "We panicked. I closed the door on the stall. Jemma was wearing gloves, so no fingerprints, but we tried to hide the shovel, anyway." Samar shot Cindy a dark look. "Jemma said we should tell her mother—that she'd know what to do."

Everyone's gaze swung to Cindy.

She momentarily cringed under the pressure, then pressed her lips together and gathered herself taller. She gazed at the detectives over Jemma's head and continued to rub her daughter's back. "Yes. My daughter told me about the horrible thing she'd done, and by then she'd noticed her signature hair ribbon had fallen out."

She shrugged. "I told them I'd handle it, like any good mother would. So I sent them to bed, headed back to the stables, and retrieved her ribbon from outside the stall."

I gawked at the way she said it all so nonchalantly.

"I'm just a mother trying to protect her daughter. Surely, you'd all do the same for your child."

Maybe. Still, if Jemma had acted in defense of Samar, surely they could have called the police and explained the situation. I crossed my arms. Except, of course, that it would've eventually led them back to Cindy stealing from Halliwell. Something just didn't seem right about this. Cindy struck me as incredibly selfish and manipulative. She'd tricked her daughter's fiancé into losing the cup to protect herself, for goodness's sake.

Detective Bennett narrowed her eyes. "Miss Watkins, you say you didn't mean to kill Timmy Pipe. Why hit him twice, then?"

Jemma lifted her wet, swollen face. "What?"

Bennett raised a brow. "Timmy Pipe was hit twice on the head."

Jemma sniffled and looked confused. "I—I didn't."

Samar nodded his agreement. "She just hit him once."

"There, there." Cindy patted her daughter's back and pulled her face back against her shoulder. "You two were probably in shock and just don't remember the second blow."

Detective Bennett narrowed her eyes and studied Cindy.

Suddenly, I realized what was wrong. "Where's the weight, Cindy?"

21

ARRESTED

All eyes swung to me, and Leo leaned over, lowering his voice. "Weight?"

I hadn't discussed this part with the guys beforehand because it'd just come to me. I shot him and Cho steady looks. "Trust me."

I turned back to Cindy. "Yes, Cindy, the lead weight." I gestured at Samar. "You said Timmy hit you with one."

He frowned and nodded. "That's right."

I turned to the detectives. "Did you find one at the crime scene?"

For the first time, a hint of a smile spread across Detective Bennett's lips. "No." She turned to face Cindy. "No, we did not."

Jemma lifted her tearstained face from her mother's shoulder and sniffled. "That's weird. Timmy was holding it when I hit him with the shovel." She turned to face the stall, which was now cordoned off by police tape. "He must've dropped it. It's got to be in there among the hay somewhere."

Detective Bennett stepped closer to Cindy, whose expression darkened. "Unless someone took it."

The horse breeder scoffed. "I don't know what you're getting at." She shrugged. "I have no idea where that weight is. Why would I?"

I stood up straighter, confident that finally, we'd figured it out. "Because you used it to kill Timmy Pipe."

Cindy scoffed out a humorless laugh and looked around the circle, from the cops to the track officials. "She's crazy." She threw a hand at me. "She's a waitress who thinks she's a detective now?" She shot me a pitying look. "Newsflash! My daughter already confessed to killing Timmy Pipe, and the police found the murder weapon—it was the shovel." She made faces at the others, trying to get them to join her in mocking me.

But I held steady—and Jack, Mim, Cho, and Leo closed ranks around me as Tilda nuzzled my ankles.

I shook my head.

Cindy turned to the detectives. "Case closed." She patted her daughter's back. "At least now your conscience can be clear."

I couldn't hold back a snort as I stepped forward. "Not quite."

Cindy shot me a dark look.

"I have a theory. When you returned to retrieve Jemma's ribbon, you looked into the stall and found Timmy Pipe alive."

Jemma sucked in a breath and stared at her mother, wide-eyed.

"Jemma injured him but didn't kill him. But you couldn't let him live, not when you knew he'd tell the world about Samar losing the race on purpose. Because that would lead to Samar confessing that he'd done it to help Jemma win because of the debt you owed Halliwell to fund your stables. Your whole world would come crashing down if you let Timmy Pipe live."

I sucked in a breath, my heart racing. "You found the heavy lead weight lying there, with Samar's blood already on it, and you used it to hit Timmy Pipe again."

"The second blow," Detective Bennett murmured.

"And that's what killed him." I turned to the detectives. "I have a hunch that if you look for that lead weight, you'll find DNA evidence for both Samar and Timmy on it. As well as Cindy's fingerprints."

Jemma gasped and covered her mouth with both hands. "I—I really didn't kill him?"

Cindy's chest heaved and she shot me a murderous look. *Yeesh.*

Jemma whirled on her mother. "You let me think I killed him this whole time?" She pressed a hand to her heart. "You knew how it was eating me up! And you're the one who killed him?" Her chest heaved.

Cindy rolled her eyes and looked up and away. "Calm down, Jemma, you look most unseemly."

Jemma's mouth fell open, the whites showing all around her wild eyes. "You were going to let me get arrested for his murder?" She let out an incredulous huff. "You're a *terrible* mother!"

Cindy spun on her heel and shot daggers at her daughter. "Oh, shut it, you spoiled little brat! I did all of this so we could have a better life!"

Jemma backed away into Samar's arms. "*You* wanted a better life, Mum, *you* did! You were going to let me go to prison and spend my whole life thinking I'd murdered someone."

Cindy glared at Jemma and Samar. "You think it's cheap,

funding a racing career, darling? Ha! When I opened my stables, the banks wouldn't lend me, a single mother, anything. So I borrowed a little."

Halliwell scoffed. "You stole from me!"

Cindy rolled her eyes. "I planned to pay you back. But horses are expensive to feed and house and train. The bills added up, so I had to keep borrowing. At that point, the only way to get out of the hole was to keep digging." Her nostrils flared. "Then you had to go and hire Gary." She jerked her head at the auditor. "Time was running out, so I had to think fast. I'd recently learned of your little romance, though you tried to hide it from me." She sneered at Jemma and Samar.

Jemma scoffed. "Yeah, because I thought you'd tell me I should be focusing on my career instead of young men."

Cindy sniffed at Samar. "I knew how smitten you were with my daughter, so I used that to my advantage. You agreed to lose so my Jemma could win the cup and we'd get the prize money to pay back Halliwell." She bared her teeth. "It was all working out until Timmy figured it out." She shrugged, eyes wild. "If my daughter had just finished him off, it would've all been fine. But no, it's always up to me to do the dirty work." She jabbed a thumb at her chest. "I had to finish what my daughter started, to keep Timmy quiet."

I planted my hands on my hips. "You started the fire at the inn too, didn't you?"

Cindy's expression grew even darker. "Halliwell called and told me you'd paid him a little visit and told him all about me and Gary spending time together." She glared at me. "I had to shut you up. I don't know how you got out alive!"

I played out that night again, clinging to the mossy roof

tiles. Thank goodness Fitz had saved me—I'd nearly perished at Cindy's hand, just like Timmy Pipe.

Detective Bennet curled her lip and looked thoroughly disgusted as she gazed at Cindy. "What happened to the murder weapon?"

Cindy rolled her eyes. "I heard someone coming, so I hastily wiped the blood off in the hay, dashed out of there and ran into one of Jemma's grooms. He took the weight off my hands and said he'd return it to the locker room." She curled her lip. "So I imagine it's there, since I haven't had an opportunity to go find it and wipe off any remaining blood and fingerprints."

Detective Bennett shook her head. "Cindy Watkins, you're under arrest for the murder of Timmy Pipe, as well as for arson and the attempted murder of Minnie Wells." She frowned. "And that's just for a start."

The uniformed officers rushed forward and cuffed Cindy's hands behind her back as Samar wrapped Jemma in a big hug.

The track officials stepped forward and addressed the jockeys. The older one frowned. "I hope you know you're both disqualified from racing until further notice. The board will be reviewing your cases."

Jemma blew out a breath. "That's the least of our worries."

Samar nodded. "I think we've had enough horses and racing for a while."

As the cops turned to go, Jemma caught Bennett's eye. "Am I being charged?"

She gave the jockey a hard look, then shook her head. "No. You were acting in defense of Samar. You had reason to believe Timmy was going to kill him."

Jemma's shoulders slumped with relief.

Bennett turned her dark gaze to Samar. "You may be facing race fixing charges...though I suspect our department may be inclined to cut you a plea deal, for your help in bringing charges against Cindy Watkins."

Samar nodded and Jemma rubbed his back, both looking somewhat reassured.

The detective turned to me and nodded. "Good work, Miss Wells."

I grinned. Coming from the stoic detective, that was high praise indeed.

22

MENDED

It felt strange to return to working the tea tent, but we still had to close out the last day of the races. I dilly-dallied while Fitz baked scones and filled him in on Cindy's arrest.

He looked up now and again, his dark eyes wide, but never interrupted me.

"And then they arrested her and said Samar and Jemma were off the hook, since she'd acted in defense of her fiancé." I shrugged. "I mean, they're probably going to need a lot of therapy." I quirked my lips to the side. "And I'm not sure the track officials will ever let them race again after their part in the Jane Austen race-fixing scandal, but it was a happy-ish ending for the young couple."

I smirked. I couldn't help that every time I mentioned Jane Austen the horse, I briefly imagined my favorite Regency author as the one caught up in a horse racing controversy.

Fitz brushed his wavy hair off his forehead with the back of his hand, leaving behind an oddly attractive smear of flour. His gaze scanned my face, lingering for a moment on my lips, before he gave me a lop-sided grin. "I've lived a long time, but never met anyone who seems to get themselves in the middle of trouble quite so often." His gaze grew warmer. "Or manages to cut to the truth of things quite so well."

My cheeks grew hot, and I dipped my gaze to my sneakers before looking back up at him with a grin. "Thanks. I think."

He chuckled as he cut scones into circles with a cookie cutter. "So now what?"

I spun around and leaned my elbows on the counter. "So now the races go on."

My eyes drifted toward the dining area of the tent. Every table out there was abuzz with news of the murder, arson, and scandal. The runner-up had taken Jemma's place, and the cup race was still set for this afternoon. I hoped the officials would take into consideration that Cindy had tricked Samar into thinking he had to lose the race to keep Jemma safe—though he was fully aware he was committing a crime himself. In any case, the young couple seemed happy to know they hadn't actually killed Timmy Pipe and weren't going to prison.

"Minnie."

I glanced up at Fitz, leaving my musings behind. "Hm?"

He licked his lips. "I feel I've barely seen you this weekend, and I find I quite miss our conversations... and you."

My cheeks warmed. "I miss you too."

His throat bobbed. "I know I was reluctant to leave Bath, but it's been a good experience for me to change things up. It's helped me realize I might've been a *bit* stuck in my ways." He grinned. "Which I know will come as a shock to you."

I smiled back.

He pinched his brows together in thought. "As much as you've inspired me, our kitchen-mate, Carmen, has as well."

Annddd, smile gone.

He pressed his lips together and looked as if he were fighting a smirk. "You may have noticed she's a bit forward with her feelings."

I shot him a flat look, and he chuckled.

"While I cannot say I return those feelings for her—"

A weight lifted off my chest.

"—there is someone I care about, and it's helped me realize perhaps I should be a bit more forward myself." His dark gaze held mine. "Would you care to join me for a cup of tea when we return to Bath?"

I grinned. "It's a d-deal." I'd almost said date, but I decided to let it be a little more casual. Fitz had told me how much I meant to him, and I believed him, but he was a mysterious, hundreds-of-years-old vampire, and I was fresh out of a divorce. We were both starting to find ourselves open to the idea of love again—but we were taking it slow.

After the pandemonium of the weekend of races, slow sounded pretty good. Also, a decent night's sleep wouldn't hurt. I longed to crawl into my soft, fluffy bed in my friend Gus's attic with Tilda.

I straightened. "Better get back to work, boss." I winked at Fitz, then lifted a tea tray covered with tasty-looking bites and headed for the dining area. Suddenly, the general roar of the crowd and blare of the announcers, which I'd learned to mostly tune out as background noise, cut into my consciousness.

The crowd gasped, women screamed, and then the stands grew quiet.

I shot a worried look at Fitz and hurried through the tent, then whirled to face the television screen.

"Oh no."

A horse lay on its side, its jockey partly pinned beneath it. I set the tea tray on the nearest table and held my hand over my mouth.

"Little Dancer's down." The announcer's voice cut through the relative hush, his normally upbeat tone more subdued. "A tragedy, a terrible tragedy. We have yet to get word of the extent of Little Dancer's injuries, but veterinary and medical staff are now arriving down on the track to give both horse and rider treatment."

I had to look away as the broadcast cut to a replay in slow motion of the horse leaping, but stumbling on the landing. It was too heartbreaking. I wished the horse and jockey would be alright, though from the looks of it, the horse had been hurt pretty badly. My stomach tightened with concern. Poor Jack and Mim; they'd been trying so hard to keep them safe.

I gasped. Jack had barely been out of police custody a few hours, and Mim had worked herself to the bone, charming the horses on the fly for the past couple of days. They needed help if they were going to heal Little Dancer. And though I had miles to go on my magic work, I might be able to do something. I had to at least try.

I dashed for the tent's exit, brushing past Leo on my way. "Sorry! I've got to go!"

"Minnie—wait!"

But there wasn't time to explain. I pushed past the line of diners waiting to be seated and jostled my way through the dense crowds until I could get a peek at the track. An ambulance pulled slowly onto the track, headed for the downed horse and rider.

I spun around and sprinted for the staff-only area.

23

A SHIFT

I pushed my way through the crowd and around to the staff entrance, flashing my badge as I dashed by. My heart pounded in my chest, and that stomach-turning moment when the horse landed wrong on its leg replayed over and over in my mind. I had to do anything I could to help.

Unfortunately, gaining admittance onto the track itself wasn't so easy. A couple of refrigerator-sized security guards in white polo shirts blocked me and a handful of press from pushing past them onto the track. Just behind them, a makeshift screen had been erected with blue plastic tarps blocking the horse from view. I knew Jack, and hopefully Mim, had to be there.

Breathless, I tried flashing my badge at the security guard with the thick mustache. "Please. Let me through."

He lifted a brow and dipped his head to better read my badge. He snorted and straightened. "Nice try. Says you're working food and beverage, so unless the horses need some tea, back it up."

I huffed. Rude. Not like I was going to be put off that

easily, though. I rose on my toes, cupped my hands to the sides of my mouth, and screamed, "Jack! Mim! It's Minnie. I want to help!"

A few reporters with cameras and recording devices shot me funny looks, but I tried again, my voice echoing around the tunnel under the bleachers. Though the crowd had quieted after the poor horse's fall, I still doubted they'd be able to hear me over all the commotion. I sucked in a breath, closed my eyes, and reached out to Mim with my mind. I didn't know if it would work—I'd never done it before. But it was worth a shot.

I'm in the tunnel. They won't let me through. I can help.

I opened my eyes and shouted again. "Mim! Jack!"

"Keep it down!" the security guard barked.

I glared at him, then glanced past his shoulder as a head of long, wiry gray hair popped out from behind the tarp. I beamed and waved my arms over my head. "Mim! Mim! Over here!"

She spotted me, then hiked up her long skirt and bustled over as quickly as she could. She tapped the guard on the shoulder, and he spun and gave her a curious look. "She's with me."

Mim reached out, grabbed my hand, and dragged me past the guards and protesting members of the press. I ignored them and dashed with Mim to the tarp, eager to help but dreading what I'd find.

"Is it bad?"

Mim's face crumpled as she jogged along beside me. She nodded, her chin quivering. "It's my fault. I let my guard down and—" The words choked in her throat as we reached the flurry of activity around the horse, which lay panting on its side. The beautiful brown creature's ribs rose and fell quickly, its eyes wild and nostrils flared.

Pity twisted my stomach, and I touched Mim's arm. "How can I help?"

Jack knelt beside its front foreleg and spared me a quick glance before ordering a few techs to hand him tools and a bag of some liquid.

"Broken leg," the grizzled veterinarian muttered. "We'll have to put her down unless we can work some magic." He glanced back and shot me a significant look.

My breath caught. No pressure or anything.

Mim fumbled for my hands and clasped them in her own. "Minnie. I'm tired. I don't have it in me, but maybe together we can save him."

I nodded. "How?"

She turned to her friend. "Jack. We need privacy."

He opened his mouth as if to protest, then looked back down at the panting horse. He dragged his rough hand down his mouth and beard, then nodded. "Everyone out!" he barked.

A young woman in vet tech scrubs gaped at him. "But Jack, we can't just leave—"

Jack pushed to his feet and cut her off. "I said out. These women are experienced professionals. We need to give them space." He spread his arms wide and ushered the several techs out. He glanced back before dipping beyond the tarp himself. "Good luck. I'll keep everyone away."

Mim nodded, her curls bouncing, then turned to me. We stood alone in the makeshift tent beside the injured horse, enclosed in four hanging walls of blue plastic tarps.

My mentor squeezed my hands. "Focus, Minnie."

I nodded and shut my eyes.

"Tune out the crowd. Listen to your breathing."

I wanted to protest that I couldn't. The murmur from the stands was too loud, my mind and heart racing too fast.

Maybe I could use that.

I felt for my heartbeat, thumping hard against my ribs, pulsing in my temples and neck. Despite feeling lightheaded with adrenaline, finding my heart helped me feel more grounded.

"Good," Mim coached, her voice shaky.

Our hands, clasped together, grew hotter.

"That's it," the older witch coaxed. "I'm going to recite a spell." Her hands tightened around mine almost painfully. "I need you to funnel magic into me to power it. You can do it, Minnie."

I wasn't sure I completely understood, but I'd do my best.

"Focus on sending your magic through my hands."

Eyes still closed against the outside world, I tried to focus and ground myself, to channel my power.

"Ready?"

I gulped. No, but I didn't have a choice. I nodded. "Ready."

Mim blew out a shaky breath.

"Race, race, keep apace,
Horse of strength and equine grace,
Though you fell, you shall not fall,
Death is near, but shall not call,
Mend, mend, 'tis not the end,
'Twas not a break, but just a bend."

Our hands grew so hot they stung, but Mim squeezed mine and I refused to let go or give up until I'd given it my all. She started her spell again, and I joined in with her, my eyes squeezed shut tight.

"Race, race, keep apace,
Horse of strength—"

We muttered the spell together through gritted teeth as the rest of the world fell away. There was only heat in my hands and our voices melding together in a rhythmic chant.

"Mend, mend, 'tis not the end—"

I gritted my teeth as my hands trembled and the heat grew almost unbearable. I focused on the rhyme, on channeling my magic to Mim. Was it enough? Could we heal the poor horse's leg and keep it from being killed?

Suddenly, relief swept over me like a cool breeze. The sweat on my neck grew chilly, and I let out a relieved sigh. Mim squeezed my hands, and I returned to chanting the spell—but it was easier now. The heat in our hands was a soothing warmth instead of a burning one. I sensed magic coursing through me, into Mim, and from her to the horse.

"Death is near, but shall not call,
Mend, mend, 'tis not the end—"

. . .

The horse whickered and let out a contented sigh. Our voices grew stronger, more confident.

"'Twas not a break, but just a bend."

Mim released my hands—or maybe they flew apart. I sucked in a breath and fluttered open my eyes. It took me a few blinks to regain my bearings, to hear the soft roar of the crowd, to catch my breath.

Mim, though pale and sweaty, managed a wry grin. "We did it."

The horse breathed easy now, its eyes calm.

Mim shrieked and threw her arms around me, enveloping me in the strong scents of frankincense and lavender. "You did it!"

I giggled, heady with our success. "I don't know how it happened. Toward the end, I was so hot and exhausted—I didn't think I could keep up much longer. Then all of a sudden, I got this cool rush of magic."

Mim's eyes darted to the side, and she froze. "Oops."

I frowned, confused, and followed her gaze. "Oh no."

Leo stood to my left, dumbfounded, with Tilda in his arms. She swished her tail side to side.

You're welcome.

Oh. So that's where that surge of power had come from. That made sense now—Tilda always amplified my magic.

Mim patted my shoulder. "I'll let you two talk." She crouched by the horse's head. "You alright, darling?" As she stroked its nose, the horse blinked and sighed happily, its gaze calm and breathing relaxed.

I turned back to face Leo and scrunched up my face in a tight smile. "So… I guess you saw all of that?"

He nodded slowly, and Tilda leapt out of his arms and trotted over to Mim. "You're… a…"

I winced. "Witch."

A puff of orange smoke and sparkles filled the air, and I let out a startled shriek.

Mim shushed me. "Don't scare the horse."

An ironic warning, considering a full-sized, shaggy-maned lion blinked at me from the place where Leo had just stood. I couldn't breathe, but in the space of a heartbeat, another explosion of sparkles and dust filled the air, and the lion disappeared—once again replaced by my friend.

He dipped his head and rubbed the back of his neck. "Sorry."

I had no words.

"I should probably explain. Tilda started freaking out after you ran out of the tent, so I scooped her up and followed you. We saw you head down here on TV." He let out a nervous chuckle. "Jack got us past security and… well, here we are. That was a big surprise—you being a witch. Really triggered me, I guess."

"I—triggered—you into—" I stammered, my brain not computing.

He's a lion shifter.

I glanced down as Tilda threaded between my ankles.

"You knew?"

Leo chuckled. "Can you talk to her?"

I looked up. "Yeah, lately." I rolled my eyes. "Not entirely sure I like it."

You love it.

Mim chuckled from her spot by the horse's head. "Leo the lion?"

The butler shrugged his stocky shoulders. "My parents were very literal." He lifted his nose and sniffed. "I knew you smelled different, but I've never met a witch before." He looked off to the side. "Huh. So that's what one smells like."

"I just—" I shook my head and dragged my hands through my hair. "First of all, I didn't know shifters existed."

He nodded. "We do." Leo tipped his head to the side. "You know, it's funny, because with Fitz, I'd never smelled a vampire before either, but I knew right away what he was. Go figure."

I glanced behind me at Mim—it was now her turn to be shocked. "Yeah, Fitz is a vampire... don't say anything?"

She shook her head. "Not a word."

I turned back to Leo. "Does Fitz know you know?"

He shook his head. "I don't think so.

"Does he know what you are?"

"I doubt it."

"Do the other butlers know?"

He grinned. "Really? You think Cho puzzled this out?" He shook his head. "Not a chance."

I blew out a heavy breath. "Oh boy. Well... this changes things."

Mim snorted. "Maybe not that much. Come on—let's get this guy back on his feet."

As if on cue, the horse rolled to his side and, though a little unsteady, rose to his feet, shook his head, and took a few steady steps right out from under the tarp. Mim and I chuckled, then dashed out after him, with Leo and Tilda on our heels. Jack and the vet techs rushed over. The veterinarian swept Mim into his arms and swirled her around, peppering her with kisses.

I grinned. I knew they were more than just friends.

The techs gaped at Mim and me. The young woman

who'd protested having to leave the horse with us gently poked and prodded its formerly injured leg. "I checked it myself—this leg was broken." Her mouth hung open as she turned to me and Mim. "It's totally healthy now. How did—what did you—I don't under—"

Jack left Mim and ushered the young woman to the side. "Calm down. I'll explain everything—"

"How's he going to explain this?"

She shrugged. "I don't know. Probably tell her we used some new age mumbo jumbo." She winked. "Most humans like to have everything explained in a neat little box. They're more than happy to write off something unexplainable as a strange fluke and move on. And if that doesn't work, we can help out with a little magic." She wiggled her fingers.

Leo sidled up beside me and threw a thick arm around my shoulders. I looked between him and Mim, taking my mentor's hand.

"Well, after what I just saw"—I flashed my eyes at Leo—"I can understand the desire to write off the unexplainable."

He chuckled. "Oh, Minnie, hold your horses. This has been a wild weekend, but I'm sure with time, you'll be able to rein in your shock."

I shot him a flat look as he, Mim, Tilda, and I walked off the track together. "Enough with the horse puns."

He smirked. "You want me to quit horsing around? I say neigh."

"Urg!" I couldn't help but chuckle. "Stop! These are terrible!"

Even Mim snickered.

"I know you think I'm *foal* of it..." Leo waggled his brows. "But I can't wait to hoof it back to Bath."

"That's it." I slugged his arm, and he recoiled.

"Hay!" He leaned close. "Get it? Hay?"

I threw my head back and groaned. “Make it stop!”

But in truth, the silliness helped me feel more normal while I dealt with the utter strangeness of discovering Leo was a shifter. While I was probably still going to be reeling from that knowledge for a while, I’d never felt more empowered in my magic or supported by my friends. Besides, Fitz and I had a date planned. I resisted the urge to squeal and do my happy dance. While it’d been a crazy weekend indeed, the change of scenery seemed to have unlocked new depths in me—and my friendships.

OTHER BOOKS BY ERIN JOHNSON

The Magical Tea Room Mysteries

Minnie Wells is working her marketing magic to save the coziest, vampire-owned tea room in Bath, England. But add in a string of murders, spells to learn, and a handsome Mr. Darcy-esque boss, and Minnie's cup runneth over with mischief and mayhem.

Spelling the Tea
With Scream and Sugar
A Score to Kettle
English After-Doom Tea

The Spells & Caramels Paranormal Cozy Mysteries

Imogen Banks is struggling to make it as a baker and a new witch on the mysterious and magical island of Bijou Mer. With a princely beau, a snarky baking flame and a baker's dozen of hilarious, misfit friends, she'll need all the help she can get when the murder mysteries start piling up.

Seashells, Spells & Caramels
Black Arts, Tarts & Gypsy Carts

Mermaid Fins, Winds & Rolling Pins
Cookie Dough, Snow & Wands Aglow
Full Moons, Dunes & Macaroons
Airships, Crypts & Chocolate Chips
Due East, Beasts & Campfire Feasts
Grimoires, Spas & Chocolate Straws
Eclairs, Scares & Haunted Home Repairs
Bat Wings, Rings & Apron Strings
* Christmas Short Story: Snowflakes, Cakes & Deadly Stakes

The Magic Market Paranormal Cozy Mysteries

A curse stole one witch's powers, but gave her the ability to speak with animals. Now Jolene helps a hunky police officer and his sassy, lie-detecting canine solve paranormal mysteries.

Pretty Little Fliers
Friday Night Bites
Game of Bones
Mouse of Cards
Pig Little Lies
Breaking Bat
The Squawking Dead
The Big Fang Theory

The Winter Witches of Holiday Haven

Running a funeral home in the world's most merry of cities has its downsides. For witch, Rudie Hollybrook, things can feel a little isolating. But when a murder rocks the festive town, Rudie's special skills might be the one thing that can help bring the killer to justice!

Cocoa Curses
Solstice Spirits

Magical Renaissance Faire Mysteries

Trapped in a magical Renaissance Faire and accused of murder. Huzzah!

When Adelaide "Laidey" Ryan dragged herself off the couch for a date at the Renaissance Faire, she didn't expect to run into her cheating ex-fiancé. The day only gets better when she winds up trapped on the magical grounds and discovers she's a witch. And the best part? She's charged with a homicide she didn't commit.

Much A'Broom About Nothing

Special Collections

The Spells & Caramels Boxset Books 1-3

Pet Psychic Mysteries Boxset Books 1-4

Pet Psychic Mysteries Boxset Books 5-8

Want to hang out with Erin and other magical mystery readers?

Come join Erin's VIP reader group on Facebook: **Erin's Bewitching Bevy**. It's a cauldron of fun!

GET YOUR FREE NOVELLA!

A magical academy. A suspicious death. Can an inexperienced cop expose the deadly secrets lurking behind bewitched classroom doors?

Download Saved by the Spell for FREE to solve a mystical murder today!

ABOUT THE AUTHOR

A native of Arizona, Erin loves her new home in the Pacific Northwest! She writes paranormal cozy mystery novels. These stories are mysterious, magical, and will hopefully make you laugh.

When not writing, she's hiking, napping with her dogs, and losing at trivia night.

You can find Erin at her website, **www.ErinJohnsonWrites.com** or on **Facebook.** Please email her at **erin@erinjohnsonwrites.com**. She loves to hear from readers!

❀ Created with Vellum

Made in United States
Orlando, FL
22 July 2022